June Lerina Woodward was born in South Wales and brought up there and on Lundy Island. She has travelled widely, including living and working in the Austrian Tirol for several years in the 1960s and 80s. She now lives in Canterbury and has two daughters and five grandchildren.

TIROLU

June Lerina Woodward

Book Guild Publishing
Sussex, England

First published in Great Britain in 2008 by
The Book Guild
Pavilion View
19 New Road
Brighton, BN1 1UF

Typesetting in Baskerville by
Keyboard Services, Luton, Bedfordshire

Printed in Great Britain by
Athenaeum Press Ltd, Gateshead

A catalogue record for this book is available from
The British Library

ISBN 978 1 84624 283 0

1

It was the middle of September and Amelia awoke to the sound of cowbells. She opened the French windows, stood outside on the balcony and gazed at the cows and goats grazing on the lush green grass in the field below. Beyond the sloping field and farmhouse was a dip, and then on the opposite side of the narrow valley was a chairlift to the ski area that was also used in the summer by hikers. To the left and a quarter of a mile away was the village of Bachl, nestling prettily among the three surrounding mountains. The sky was azure and there was not a breath of wind. The hotel balcony was ablaze with flowers – that you could not get a pin between – in window-boxes that took up the length and width. It was in complete contrast to her home town of Exeter.

Amelia had found out a few weeks earlier that her fiancé Alex, whom she was supposed to have been marrying the following spring, had been having an affair. What made it worse was that it was with Rose, the well known 'bike' of Exeter! The source of her information was an anonymous letter sent to her from someone who did not like what was going on and obviously thought Amelia should know. She thought it was a malicious prank until she confronted Alex, who at first denied it then admitted it was just a harmless fling and long over. From that very moment Amelia saw him through different eyes and would never trust him again. Humiliated and hurt, she had broken off the engagement despite his pleas of how sorry he was, that he loved only her and to give him another chance to prove how much he meant it. It had fallen on deaf ears. After telling her parents, who were also shocked, and her friends, who weren't – as they all seemed to know but no one had the heart to tell her – she decided she was going to have to get away.

She worked as secretary to a bank manager and still had holidays due to her. After hearing the circumstances he readily agreed to her taking a fortnight's holiday, starting from the following week. In her lunch break she made her way to a travel agent. Whilst awaiting her turn her eyes fell upon a 'Lakes and Mountains' brochure and by the time an assistant became free she had already decided where she wanted to go – Bachl, described in the brochure as: 'A charming, friendly and pretty little village in the Austrian Tirol with houses and hotels built in the traditional wooden chalet style with overhanging eaves and carved balconies. There is a lively but informal night life and there are opportunities for trips out to other areas in Austria and also northern Italy. It is a popular walking area in the summer with numerous planned routes.' Little did she know that on that balmy August day in 1964, the choice of her holiday location would change the whole course of her life.

Perfect! Exactly what she wanted. She booked the holiday on the spot for the following Saturday and then went and told her parents. Eileen and Charles were a little taken aback as Amelia had never been on holiday alone before. Was she sure this was what she wanted?

'Please do not worry about me I am a big girl now. I think I was lucky to find out Alex had a roving eye before rather than after we married, and this holiday will help me get used to the idea of no longer being engaged.'

Her father looked at her seriously and said, 'Mel, you are a beautiful, gifted and kind young woman. You are barely twenty-two and with the world at your feet, so I say good riddance to that scoundrel. I wasn't particularly taken with him anyway!'

'Thanks Dad. Alex and I probably got together too young and perhaps it was never meant to be, but while I've got great parents like you and so many good friends, who needs Alex!'

Her holidays had usually been to France, so she was excited at the thought of a new challenge, especially travelling on her own. There were only seven others with her travel company booked for the Krone hotel, the rest choosing somewhere nearer the village centre. But this was exactly what she wanted and she was not disappointed by the rustic hotel and friendly staff. After a huge breakfast of fruit, yoghurt, a wide and varied selection of meats and cheeses and the best crusty bread rolls she had ever tasted, she decided to do a recce of the village and find the tourist office. As it was nearing the end of the season there were few tourists around, and those that were appeared to be mostly German or Austrian. As she passed the hikers they all nodded and said what sounded like 'Great Scot!' She had replied with *'Guten Tag'* thanks to her school A-level German but was puzzled by their greeting.

At the tourist office she met the manager Franz Rissbacher who welcomed her and was very eager to give her any help. 'Firstly,' she said, 'I am rather puzzled by the people I have passed on the way here who all appeared to be saying "Great Scot" to me and wondered if you could enlighten me?' Franz and his two assistants, Anna and Heidi, burst out laughing, which puzzled Amelia all the more until Franz explained that what they were actually saying was *'Gruss Gott'* which was the traditional Tirolean greeting. Amelia felt a bit of a lemon but Franz soon put her at ease after telling her she wasn't the first or the

3

last British person to query *'Gruss Gott'*. She found Franz and the girls very helpful, and by the time she left she was armed with lots of pamphlets, maps, and general information.

She decided she would have a coffee and entered the Hotel Post feeling a bit conspicuous as everyone else appeared to be talking either in German or what she thought was probably dialect. Her school German was adequate for a limited conversation, so after seating herself at a corner table she felt very pleased with herself to have ordered *'Eine Tasse Kaffee mit Milch bitteschon'*. She proceeded to focus her attention on the English translation of her village information and brochures. Stopping to drink her coffee her eyes wandered around the room. Everything seemed to be carved, including the ornate panels of the walls on which hung swatches of dried flowers and antlers. Every table had a little vase of fresh flowers and the waitresses all wore a pretty dirndl, the traditional Austrian dress.

She became aware of someone sitting at the bar staring at her. He was one of the most handsome men she had ever seen in her life. He smiled, which took her aback for a moment, then she quickly averted her eyes back to her pamphlets. She found it extremely difficult to stop herself taking another peep ... until temptation took over! She could have kicked herself because he was still staring at her and once again smiled. She quickly dropped her eyes back to the pamphlets. The handsome stranger suddenly appeared at her table, held out his hand and said, 'Hello! My name's Marcus. Welcome to Bachl.'

Amelia could not refuse to shake his hand and in doing so found herself looking into beautiful laughing green eyes. Oh hell's bells, what do I do now, she thought. So she quickly scooped up her literature, said 'Nice to have met you,' headed confidently for the door, tripped over

4

the door jamb and found herself in the kitchen! With a few mumbled words of apology to the kitchen staff she straightened her back and, head held high, made her way through the bar and out of the front door, leaving a puzzled and bemused Marcus to return to the bar.

Walking quickly along the road she reproached herself for her schoolgirlish behaviour and put it down to the recent upheaval of her broken engagement. 'That poor chap must think I'm a bit of a weirdo, all he did was introduce himself because he probably felt sorry for me on my own,' she thought and tried to put it to the back of her mind. She was looking forward to the next day's excursion and made a mental note to avoid the Post for a few days.

Walking towards the pick-up point to join her coach, horror of horrors – she saw Marcus standing on the balcony of a big house that she had to pass. He waved and called out, 'Good morning!' She acknowledged him with a wave back and hoped to goodness she didn't trip again as she hurriedly approached the coach. 'Stop it you silly fool, he is only being friendly,' she angrily told herself and boarded the coach. The driver was a pleasant little man with a round ruddy face and a pot belly, but he had difficulty trying to say Fraulein Carrington as he read the passenger list. 'Please call me Amelia,' she told him with a smile to which he replied, 'Welcome on the trip, Milli!' This amused Amelia and she quickly bonded with this dear little man.

By the time everyone was on board she had noticed that nearly all had German-sounding names. This was confirmed when the driver introduced himself as Georg and said that he was taking them to Krimml waterfalls, and because there were German and English on board he would be doing the commentary in both languages. Anticipating the lovely day ahead Amelia sat back in her seat and felt at peace with the world. As the coach travelled down the steep, winding mountain road, negotiating many hairpin bends, Georg gave a long, running commentary in German that only took a few minutes when it came to the English version. She realised then that his English was limited but he was doing his best, besides she found she could follow quite a bit of the German version. They passed many little villages and traversed many more hairpin bends. The scenery was breathtaking and Amelia felt so pleased with herself that she had chosen to come to the Tirol, especially Bachl which she had fallen instantly in love with.

On arrival at Krimml Amelia looked in awe at the three cascading stages of the waterfall and managed to climb the steep path to the second level. She felt light-headed and totally relaxed. Back at the foot of the Falls was a restaurant where she sat on the terrace and ordered a hot chocolate and Apfel Strudel. She was joined by Georg who asked if she was enjoying the excursion, followed by, 'Why are you on your own Milli?'

'This was a last minute booking Georg, I had a bit of an upset and wanted to get away on my own and I am so glad I chose your beautiful village,' she replied.

Noticing the change in her expression he guessed it was something to do with a boyfriend and didn't try to pursue it. She was such a pretty, pleasant little thing, he wondered how on earth any man could let her slip through his fingers. He looked thoughtful, then said, 'It is our twenty-fifth wedding anniversary and we are having a big party tonight at the Bergblick, and I was wondering if you would like to join us?' Amelia was so surprised by the invitation she didn't know quite what to say. 'My wife Trudi and our three daughters would be delighted if you

6

could join us and it would give you a chance to meet the villagers and see how the "Bachlers" celebrate,' he said happily.

'Thank you so much Georg, how could I refuse such an honour,' she replied, still a little stunned but feeling quite excited by the prospect.

'Good, I will pick you up at seven-thirty from your hotel and will make sure one of my daughters drives you back afterwards. Now it is time to get back to the bus.'

Amelia felt elated to be invited to such an important event by someone who until that morning she had never met before. She was already drawn to his kindness and sense of humour.

Hair freshly washed, make-up carefully applied and wearing her favourite blue dress, she earned a wolf whistle from Georg as he picked her up 7.30 on the dot from her hotel. At the Bergblick she was introduced to his wife Trudi, and their daughters Elsa, Maria and Hanelore. They made a great fuss of her and took her under their wing, seating her next to them at the top table. Everyone was so friendly and she found she was being treated like a bit of a celebrity. She was introduced to their many friends as 'Milli from England' and found her German, though not spectacular, was adequate to converse. The band played lovely melodies both German and Tirolean and every so often there would be spontaneous yodelling. Amelia was loving it and more on the dance floor than off.

As she was chatting to Trudi she noticed her eyes being distracted, and following her gaze looked up and saw Marcus standing there holding out his hand. 'Would you like to dance?' he asked expectantly. She could feel her colour rise and tried to appear at ease as he swept her onto the floor. 'How are you finding Bachl?' he asked after a short while – just as Amelia was wondering if he was ever going to speak.

'I'm loving it, thank you Marcus, and glad I booked two weeks' holidays instead of one.'

He made small talk but was a perfect gentleman and also an accomplished dancer as she had noticed all the men were. She had also noticed there were no 'wallflowers' as seemed to be the format in England and all the men were up and choosing a partner as soon as the band started playing – this continued for the whole evening.

Seated next to Trudi again she was a little disturbed to hear that Marcus was the Casanova of the village but didn't bother with village girls only holidaymakers, and was a bit of a heartbreaker. Trudi laughed as she warned Amelia to 'Watch out!' Amelia laughed too and said the last thing on her mind was a holiday romance and that she had come to Bachl to get away from all that. This had confirmed Georg's guess when he had told his wife about the little English girl. Trudi went on to tell her that Marcus was much revered by the village folk as he was the only boy from Bachl to go to university and not only was he clever but a beautiful tailor and in much demand. Amelia said he seemed very pleasant but rather too sure of himself.

'He was Gertraud's last child at the age of forty-eight and the only son. His six sisters and parents spoiled him rotten, and probably with so much attention at home he never had a need to get married. He must be twenty-nine now,' Trudi said after a little thought.

Armed with this information Amelia decided she was going to give him a wide berth for the rest of the holiday. She danced with so many of the village men, including Franz Rissbacher and as she was swirled around the floor she wondered what her friends would say if they could see her now. Marcus didn't ask her for another dance which she was relieved about, and after one of the most enjoyable evenings of her life Georg drove her home. As she undressed, her thoughts went back to the fantastic evening and the warmth and friendliness of the villagers – she would never forget this as long as she lived.

The days flew by and after Amelia had been on several excursions she decided she was going to spend the rest of her holiday in and around the village. She had gone into the tourist office to buy some postcards when Franz appeared from his office on hearing her voice and asked if she was having a nice time. She told him she loved the scenery, the food and the friendliness and cleanliness of the village and added she was going to come down to earth with a bump when she returned to England. Franz had discreetly coaxed out of her what life entailed for her in England so she had told him about Exeter, her parents' hotel, and her work. She didn't notice that Franz appeared thoughtful and was taking it all in. He told her it was not so peaceful in the ski season but a hive of activity, as Bachl was quickly becoming a very popular resort. Amelia told him she would love to see it in the winter and hoped to come back in the middle of March when her next holiday was due. Franz asked her if she could pop in the following day as there was something he wanted to ask her. 'Certainly,' she told him but wondered what on earth he wanted to know, and why not today?

The next morning as Amelia sat, Franz explained that as Bachl was becoming a very popular ski resort with the Brits now, there was a problem concerning the ski instructors' lack of the English language which meant that quite a few of them could not instruct British guests. He went on to explain that they all had a smattering – some could speak more than others but they all needed English classes – and that he had tried to teach them the basics but found they were not taking him seriously. Wondering where this was going, Amelia nodded, and listened intently as Franz told her he had a large house that was used as an annexe to the Hotel Krone in the winter season which meant that there was only himself and his housekeeper Frieda in between seasons. Totally lost, Amelia nodded once again, but started to see the picture emerging as Franz explained he thought it would be a good idea if he could get an English person to teach the boys for ten weeks in return for free accommodation and a small wage.

She thought for a moment and told him she would love to be able to help but she did not know of anyone to fit the bill as all her friends were in full-time work, but there must be someone somewhere who would jump through hoops for an opportunity like this. She was left open-mouthed when Franz told her he had found the person and she was sitting right opposite him! Before she had chance to say anything further, Franz said he wanted her to think it over carefully before giving him her answer. Amelia assured him she would be back later that afternoon but could not promise anything at that moment as it had caught her completely off guard. She left the office with her mind racing, her first reaction being that it would be madness giving up a good job – which is what she had to do – to be able to take on this temporary work.

She walked deep in thought to a Gasthof above the village and sat on the terrace overlooking the peaceful scene of the red-roofed spiral church that was in the centre of Bachl, surrounded by chalet-style houses and hotels, fields and mountains. It was gloriously warm, with the hum of the bees taking pollen from the abundant colourful mass of flowers in the window-boxes, birdsong, cowbells and occasional yodelling coming from somewhere in the distance. With an ice-cold mineral water in her hand she gazed at the view and felt so happy, relaxed, and strangely at home. She had almost made up her mind when the deciding factor came in the shape of the whole family that had come out on the terrace to shake her hand, introduce themselves and welcome her. They told her they too had been at Georg and Trudi's party and were obviously genuinely delighted to meet her. There were a lot of people at that party so Amelia was at a great advantage having met so many of the locals in such a short space of time and whereas she could not remember all their names, they certainly knew her!

Yes! Yes! Yes was going to be her answer. She reasoned that with her qualifications it would not be difficult to find another job in Exeter but she would never get an opportunity like this again. She knew it was not going to be easy convincing her parents of that – especially her father – but they would soon come around to the idea. Franz was in the main office when she arrived back and had an expectant look on his face as he said, 'Well Milli, are you going to tell me what I want to hear?' She smiled broadly and said 'Yes.' Franz, Heidi and Anna all beamed and told her how much they looked forward to her return in the second week of October. Franz was obviously relieved to hand this particular responsibility over to her and told her it would also benefit her in improving her already wide knowledge of the German language. She refused to think beyond what would happen when this course was completed but she knew she was going to enjoy every moment she was here. It was a great privilege and one she could most certainly not miss.

The next few days passed very quickly and it seemed that the villagers had heard and obviously approved of the arrangement. She saw Marcus often. He made no attempt to approach her again but always gave her a cheeky smile. She was feeling a mixture of being flattered but very wary of his attention and she definitely did not want to encourage him. Trudi had told her he had a thriving business with his sports shop and tailoring business but spent far too much time in the Gasthofs. Amelia shook her head and remarked what a very foolish man, but there must be some reason for him to constantly seek solace in the Gasthofs. Trudi replied that his mother and sisters nagged him for wasting too much time away from his business which would promptly send him out again, creating a 'vicious circle'.

2

The day of departure arrived and after her farewells Amelia boarded the coach for the transfer to Munich airport. It was over a two-hour journey away, and once in the valley and travelling further and further away from Bachl she found her spirits becoming lower and lower. She felt an air of panic at leaving this safe haven where she had felt so happy and at home. She then started to doubt whether she would really be coming back. Was it too good to be true? Could she handle it? Was she doing the right thing? What if at the English classes the men didn't take her seriously? What would her parents and friends think and would they try to discourage her? More importantly, what if her employer insisted she worked out the obligatory one month's notice? All these thoughts mulled through her mind until she forced herself to stop panicking over things that might not happen, but the niggle persisted and she could not shake it off.

Her parents met her at Exeter airport and noticed straight away the change in her. She was her old happy-go-lucky self and not the same downhearted daughter they had waved off a few short weeks ago. She enthusiastically told them of the wonderful village and its people and how much she had loved it all, but decided to wait until they arrived home before dropping the bombshell. Sitting with her parents and enjoying a nice cup of tea she gently broached the subject of her plans. Much as they were going to miss her, and much as they did not like the idea of her giving up her work, they were so relieved to see the old sparkle and sense of humour had returned they accepted her decision and wished her well.

Her friends enthusiastically welcomed her home and were more than a little envious to hear of her plans for the next three months, but their main concern was what she would do on her return. She told them she would worry about that when the time came, but in the meantime she was certainly not going to miss an opportunity like this by worrying about the future. She pointed out that the previous month her future had been already planned – she was marrying Alex in the spring, buying a home, having kids and living happy ever after! Now she was free, independent and looking forward to the future.

'Talking about Alex, how is the pathetic cheat?' she asked. The reply was he had really regretted his indiscretion with Rose and was hoping against hope she had forgiven him, put the past to one side and could make a fresh start. She instructed her friends to tell him he was out of her life completely, in fact she had hardly thought of him at all, but that when she had it was not with affection! They drank a toast to her new adventure and told her she would be missed but they looked forward to her return and hearing the next episode of her time in Bachl. Her employer understood the situation as he had already heard of her broken engagement and because of this he agreed to her two weeks' notice instead of the statutory month, but also told her if there was a vacancy in the bank in the future she would be top of the list.

Her two weeks at home were spent working out her notice and sorting out three months of clothing, and other arrangements including her finances. Realising her luggage was too heavy for a flight she made enquiries about travelling by train. She was delighted to find there was a train from Victoria Continental Railway every day at 3 pm that involved going to Dover, crossing on the ferry and joining the Arlberg Express at Calais at 8 pm, arriving the following day at noon in Innsbruck.

She booked her ticket and couchette and was waved off by her parents at Exeter station for the first lap of her journey. Arriving at Calais, she found herself allocated a couchette with a Swiss girl who was travelling to Basle. They hit it off straight away, both being pleased no one else was sharing the four-berth compartment. Amelia's new-found friend was called Eloise, who had been spending two weeks' holiday with her aunt in London. She worked in a travel agency in Basle and spoke excellent English. They chatted away until well after midnight, with Amelia feeling happy and lucky to have such a nice companion.

As the train zoomed through northern France they finally dropped off to sleep and were awoken by a knock on the door. Opening the blinds they saw it was daylight and outside their door was a tray of coffee and croissants. As they ate their breakfast Amelia gazed in awe at the dramatic change of scenery. The depressing and flat scenery of northern France had, in stark contrast, been replaced by pretty wooden chalets with balconies, rivers and fir trees, with a backdrop of high mountains and snow-capped peaks. Late morning, as they continued to chat away they realised that the train was approaching Basle so Eloise hurriedly got her luggage together. Amelia quickly took her address and wrote it on her magazine to transfer into her address book later. With the panic to get out into the corridor to the exit, Eloise did not have time to take down Amelia's address but was told that once in Bachl her friend would send a postcard with the details. Amelia was sorry to see her leave and told her that if ever she had a little girl she would call her Eloise and hope she would be as sweet, pretty and unspoilt as her namesake. Promising to keep in touch with each other

Eloise stood on the platform and waved until the train was out of sight.

The train arrived at Innsbruck and the waiting car of Franz Rissbacher. As they drove along the Inn Valley Franz chatted about Bachl and its inhabitants. He explained it was now out of season, the hotels and restaurants were closed for renovation in preparation for the busy ski season, with only one Gasthof remaining open. He pointed out that she would be the only English girl in the village and was sure she would not be bored. At the Rissbacherhof he introduced her to his housekeeper Frieda, who only spoke a limited amount of English but was eager to learn more which meant that between them they could help each other. Once settled into her en-suite room with huge balcony overlooking the fields that would become the nursery slopes, Amelia knew she was going to enjoy every single minute of the next three months.

Over dinner Franz told her how happy and relieved he was to hand over the responsibility of the English classes. Amelia replied that she was looking forward to the challenge and hoped the ski instructors were too. The first of the twice-weekly classes started that very Friday, which gave her two days to get herself organised and reacquaint herself with Bachl. She felt euphoric and so grateful to have this fantastic opportunity. It seemed like another planet and her very own Utopia. There was no doubt in her mind that she was going to have a completely new and wonderful experience. She thought if she had a glass of wine at that very moment she would be as high as a kite!

After breakfast the next morning she wandered into the village and the Spar supermarket. The locals were mildly amused at her presence but their warmth and enthusiasm at the important post she was taking over was genuine. Purchases complete, she dropped her shopping off at the Rissbacherhof and headed out of the village towards the higher pastures and wooded area. Passing the first old farmhouse she noticed several people sitting outside in the glorious October sunshine. They beckoned her to join them and she was handed a steaming mug of coffee followed by an open sandwich of home-made bread, topped with home-cured ham – it was delicious. Their command of English was zero but with her reasonable German and the use of her hands she managed a sort-of conversation. The farmer and his family spoke in dialect that had no comparison to her spoken German but they seemed to make each other understood. Amelia spent a happy hour, with the conversation entailing lots of nods and smiles. She hoped she was nodding at the right times. She found that after a generous measure of farmhouse Schnapps the conversation flowed nicely, but she didn't really enjoy the bitter taste – although the second did taste better than the first!

At the next farmhouse a quarter of a mile further up the valley the children playing outside ran up to her, took her hand and led her into the old house. The first thing that hit her was the smell of animals in the hallway. It was a mixture of hay, pigs, horses and cows, but in the kitchen there was the unmistakable aroma and warmth of a wood-burning stove. Seated around the huge table were the farmer and his wife, the grandparents and more children, all drinking coffee and eating fruit bread. They didn't seem at all surprised and welcomed her, pulling out a chair and inviting her to join them. Another cup of steaming coffee was brought to the table and a slice of the buttered fruit bread placed in front of her. They knew who she was because their eldest son was a ski instructor who would be attending her classes. After a lot of nodding and smiling again she explained that as it was getting late she should really be getting back to the village, and after another Schnapps and plenty of handshaking she happily trundled back to the Rissbacherhof. When Franz heard of her interesting afternoon he explained she was a bit of a celebrity in the village and because Bachl was becoming increasingly popular with the Brits in the ski season it was of the utmost importance the instructors learnt the appropriate English.

Franz explained the hotels and guest houses were fully booked for the Christmas and New Year, followed by a quieter few weeks and then more or less fully booked until the middle of March, when it became low season until April. The farmhouses were used as annexes to the hotels during the busy part of the season, which provided a substantial income for the families. He also explained that as per Austrian custom the cow-shed was incorporated within the farmhouse, which provided shelter for the animals and was a source of central heating. It was also more practical for the farmers to have easy access to them without having to face the elements. He told her that they cured their own bacon, baked their own bread and that every farmhouse had a still in their cellar for Schnapps burning. It was another old Austrian custom and quite legal. The Schnapps was pure with no additives and also had a medicinal quality. In summer it cools the system when you have been sweating and in winter does the reverse – a tot of Schnapps when you were cold would warm you from the end of your nose to the tips of your toes! Whether it worked or not Amelia wasn't sure, but it was a lovely thought. Most Schnapps were made from apples or pears, which were in good supply in the summer. However the more expensive ones were made from wild berries, apricots, cherries, elderberries and many other fruits, but like all alcohol, too many would render you senseless. Amelia found all of this information fascinating.

After dinner Franz went through the lists of words and

phrases that were the most important to the instructors – not just to speak but also to understand questions and be able to respond. There would be 22 in her class and Franz had already informed them that not only must they speak English at the classes but also whenever they met Amelia socially and when they spoke to him. The classes would be held in the school and would be from 7 until 9.30 every Monday and Friday evening. There would be a 15-minute coffee break provided by the tourist office and freshly made by Frieda his housekeeper.

It all sounded straightforward and Amelia was looking forward to meeting the instructors, however she felt just a little apprehensive. As Friday approached she was losing her confidence and allowing herself to get increasingly nervous, doubting her ability to teach. What if they didn't take her seriously? She was glad that Franz was going to be there for the first lesson and to introduce her to the men.

She arrived early to familiarise herself with the surroundings and found there were already several people there including four girls who she quickly found out were instructors for the children. They greeted her with such enthusiasm that by the time Franz and the others arrived she was quite relaxed. Amelia knew how important these lessons were to them as without spoken English they could not become instructors. All came prepared with pens and notepads and after a short introduction by Franz the lessons began. By the time the coffee break arrived Amelia felt she had missed her vocation in life, as it gave her great satisfaction and such pleasure teaching her eager pupils. There were many laughs at pronunciation – some found it easier than others – but all in all it was going very well.

After the break there was a late arrival – Marcus. He

apologised for his lateness but explained he had just returned from his holiday in Sweden, he then joined in with the rest, listening intently to every word she spoke. She had wondered why she had not seen him around the village and now knew why. He already had a good command of the English language and was keen to learn more but Amelia was wary of him. She reproached herself for this as the poor chap was only being friendly, but she had to admit to herself – he unnerved her!

At the end of the lesson they all thanked her and the four girls – Resi, Gretl, Lisl and Hanelore – invited her to join them in the Hotel Post for a drink before she went home. She spent a lovely hour listening to stories of Bachl and its people and was given an insight into what happened in the ski season. It all sounded so exciting she made a promise to herself she would come back for certain in March, but in the meantime she was going to enjoy every single day she was there.

3

The following day she caught the Postbus to the valley where she picked up the train to Innsbruck. She walked from the station down Maria Theresien Strasse passing the Triumphal Arch into the long, wide street full of shops of every description. It led her into the Old Town area with its narrow cobbled streets and yet more shops and wonderful restaurants in the old rustic buildings. Even though it was out of season, there was a crowd of tourists in the square, taking photos of the Golden Roof and the very beautiful ornate buildings surrounding it. She planned to visit every week in order to see the Alpine zoo, the Patcherkofel mountain with its cable car, the Hofburg palace and gardens, the Bergisel mountain with the Olympic ski jump and so much more. She returned to Bachl tired but very happy and told Franz and Frieda of her inspirational day. Franz gave her an Innsbruck guide which he said would be useful to get herself acquainted with what to visit and how to make best use of her time there. She became so engrossed with it she awoke the next morning to find it lying next to her on her bed.

It was yet another glorious day so after breakfast she decided she would trek up the valley to the Alpenruhe Gasthof. It was a steady walk of roughly two miles and she arrived there at midday. The whole terrace was packed with locals, and Amelia found it was a popular place to visit especially on a Sunday after church. There was live music and a delicious smell of food. She glanced around and recognised many of the faces who greeted her. Georg and Trudi were there with their family and called her over to join them, ordered another plate and told her to help herself from the huge platter of Wiener Schnitzel and roast vegetables that was in the centre of the table. Georg poured her a glass of wine and toasted her return to the village. It was all a bit overwhelming and unreal. Amelia wondered yet again just what her friends would say if they could see her now. It was such a pleasant afternoon with so many people coming up to the table to welcome her back it made her feel very humble.

As she was chatting away she noticed Marcus at the far end of the terrace sitting with three other instructors playing cards. They all looked very serious. She didn't realise she had been staring until he suddenly looked up and gave her a big smile. She could have kicked herself, and casually carried on with the conversation. She was aware Marcus had stood up and was coming over to her table. He handed her a Schnapps and said, 'This is for the excellent English lesson you gave on Friday. *Prosit!*' She awkwardly accepted it, downed it and thanked him, not noticing the amused glances from a few of the locals.

The musicians playing the harp, zither and concertina were the sons of the owner. They sang and yodelled, with several of the diners joining in. It was such a happy atmosphere and the time just flew by. She walked back down to the village with Georg and his family, thanking them for a really lovely day and for making her feel so welcome, before entering the Rissbacherhof. Once indoors she sat down and brought her diary up to date and thought that one day in time to come she would be reading this and wondering if it had all really happened.

As Amelia sat on her balcony preparing the next English lesson, Frieda tapped on her door and said she had a visitor. Seeing her puzzled face Frieda explained it was

Marcus. He had his mother outside in the car and was wondering if she would accompany them to the doctor in the next village as his sisters were all busy and his mother didn't want Marcus with her in the surgery. Amelia was now even more puzzled. 'I do not even know his mother how can I possibly be of help?' Frieda replied that he was quite genuine but thought that he was acting like a lovesick schoolboy, and knowing his reputation told Amelia to go with him, not to put up with any nonsense, and to well and truly put him in his place!

Reluctantly Amelia put on her jacket and joined him outside. His mother was sitting in the back of the car and Marcus was opening the front door for her. She smiled at the old lady who said something in dialect she didn't understand. Marcus thanked her for her time and said they would be away for no longer than one and a half hours. Gingerly she asked what was wrong with his mother and his reply was 'a female thing'. Not wanting to expand on it Amelia quickly changed the subject. They made small talk during the journey and were soon in Bergbrucke. He helped his mother out of the car and proceeded to lead her into the surgery.

Amelia was just getting out of the car when Marcus reappeared and said his mother had met a friend so would not be needing her company, so instead he was going to take her for a coffee until his mother finished her visit with the doctor. Feeling well and truly conned Amelia decided to go along with it, she didn't really have a choice.

Marcus was quite chirpy and told her the Gasthof they were sitting in was the oldest in Bergbrucke and went on to explain the romantic history of the place. Without realising it she found she was hungry to hear more – it was fascinating, and she all but forgot her annoyance with him for what she thought had been a con. Perhaps after all he had been genuine, in which case she felt just a little bit ashamed of herself for being so suspicious! He behaved impeccably and when he dropped her off at the Rissbacherhof thanked her once again and drove off. It left Amelia feeling extremely stupid at thinking he had ulterior motives as it really had been a genuine request and nothing more. Still, it had been a new and unexpected experience.

At the next English lesson she felt quite relaxed and confident, and really enjoyed teaching her eager pupils. She encouraged them to ask any questions they wanted to, especially if there was something they did not understand. Immediately Johann stood up and said, 'Milli is it kitchen or chicken?' Bemused, she replied that it all depended what he was referring to, somewhere to prepare food or something he was going to eat. When he said it was something to eat she told him the easy way of defining the two was to remember he was going into the kitchen to eat some chicken.

There was a lot of laughter followed by Dieter standing up and asking, 'Is it shitting or shooting?' Amelia stifled a hysterical laugh. When she saw he was dead serious and also that the others were all awaiting the reply to this important question she replied, 'Well the only way I can relate to you the importance of using the right word in context is that one is using a gun and the other a crude English word for a bodily function: *schiessen* is shooting and *scheissen* is the other, but I advise you to forget the latter!'

The laughter was deafening and a very red-faced Dieter apologised but she knew the others had absorbed this information. 'What a bunch,' she thought to herself with a half smile.

She did not mention this little episode to Franz when she was giving him a rundown of the progress of her pupils, but was sincere in her reply to his question about whether Marcus was bothering her. She said that on the contrary, he was a star pupil and good company. 'Let's hope it stays that way,' thought Franz.

On Wednesday afternoon Lisl called on her to ask if she would like to join the crowd that evening who were going to the nine-pin bowling alley in the Ziller Valley. Amelia jumped at the chance, even though she had never been bowling before. 'Good!' said Lisl and told her she knew she would enjoy it and not to worry as she would soon pick it up. The minibus was leaving from outside the Jagerhof at 6.45 and there were usually about 14 going. They were all in high spirits, 11 men – most from her class – and Lisl and Hanelore.

As the bus trundled down the valley there were several Schnapps flasks being passed back and forth as well as bottles of lager. Amelia was really enjoying the company of this happy little crowd and was surprised when they started to sing 'Clementine' in English. The funny thing was that even though their English was limited they seem to know all the verses and she automatically joined in. But when it came to the part where Clementine had a splinter in her foot they all looked at her and went quiet when the word 'foot' should have been sung, so she found she was the only one who sang it. This was followed by manic laughter that she joined in with, thinking they had played a trick on her to get her to sing on her own – little did she know there was a meaning to the word 'foot' which she was to find out later at one of the après ski sessions!

Inside the bowling alley she was shown by Marcus how to hold the bowl – she had to cup it and put her thumb in the hole and it was a dead weight. She watched carefully as the others played so when it came to her turn, due to the Schnapps and lager, she felt quite confident. Picking up the bowl as she had been shown she bent her knees and aimed for the skittles, but failed to take her thumb out and ended up spread-eagled along the alley. She felt totally embarrassed but not for long when she realised she was being whistled and clapped. It was a hilarious evening with the team getting more and more tipsy and careless with the bowls – she was not the first or last to end up flat on her face along the alley! She laughed so much her cheekbones and ribs were aching.

The hilarity continued all the way back to Bachl. After an affectionate goodnight to her bowling pals she was still smiling as she walked back to the Rissbacherhof thinking what a fantastic evening it had been, she had never known anything even remotely like it. She also thought about Marcus, he had been quite attentive but no more so than any of the others. She loved his laughing green eyes and his sense of humour and found herself warming towards him – probably due to the alcohol she had indulged in!

4

The weeks were passing by far too quickly and she tried to put the thought of mid-December and returning to Exeter to the back of her mind. At breakfast one morning Franz asked what she planned to do when she returned home. She replied wistfully that much as she looked forward to seeing her family and friends again she hadn't really thought about work and would miss Bachl and all her new friends, but it had been one of the best experiences if not the best of her life. On hearing this, Franz came up with an idea he had been milling over for several days. 'How would you like to stay for the ski season Milli?' Completely taken aback she replied that she did not think the instructors would need her any more at the rate they were going.

'Nothing to do with instructors Milli, on the contrary, Gretl and Georg need someone to help in their Konditorei and I'm sure they would jump at the chance to employ someone who speaks fluent English as well as German. Most of the winter visitors are Brits, except at weekends when we have a huge surge of Bavarians so you would be an absolute godsend.'

It didn't take Amelia long to say how she would absolutely love it but had no experience whatsoever at working in a coffee shop. 'That's not necessary, Gretl will soon show you the ropes,' he replied, then grinned as he said, 'it's a piece of cake!' Amelia appreciated the pun, his command of the English language never ceased to amaze her. As

Franz laughed at his own joke Amelia replied it was certainly 'food for thought'. Franz, tickled by her quick reply, thought what an asset she was to the village and how lucky they were to have this gem from England in their midst. He picked up the phone and rang a delighted Gretl who asked that Amelia should go over to see them when she could.

With a spring in her step Amelia walked into the Konditorei, which was not particularly busy, and sat with Gretl and Georg to discuss her new employment. The hours were from 7.30 to 1.30 every day with one day of her choice off, enabling her to have plenty of time for skiing. As Franz had already told her, Gretl and Georg were absolutely thrilled to bits to have her working there as their English was very, very limited and she would be a great asset.

'There is only one thing Milli, we do not have accommodation here for you as all our rooms are let for the season but I will find you a room in a private house nearby,' Gretl assured her.

Amelia was absolutely over the moon at her reprieve from returning to Exeter and couldn't conceal her excitement as she rambled on about how much she was looking forward to seeing the snow and the thrill of learning to ski. When she met Lisl in the Spar in the afternoon and told her the news, Lisl's response was, 'We must celebrate! I will get a few of our friends together and we will go down the Liftstuberl this evening.'

'Great,' said Amelia and made her way to the tourist office to tell Franz that it was all sorted, except for the accommodation which Gretl seemed confident in finding for her.

The Liftstuberl was a Gasthof at the base of the chairlift ski station and roughly two miles down the valley from Bachl. A minibus was booked but so many turned up it had to make an extra trip even though it was bums on laps. The local boys loved an excuse for a night out in between seasons. Lisl had phoned ahead to let a delighted Annelies and Willi know they had a crowd coming. Out of season they only usually had weekend trade so this was a welcome party. It was a happy night with lots of laughter, singing, and, of course, booze. The revellers arrived back in the village at 2 am and a tired but very happy Amelia just fell into bed not even bothering to take off her make-up, but she did wonder why Marcus was not there.

She was awakened at 9 am by the sound of voices downstairs, followed by a loud tapping on her door. Bleary eyed, she partly opened it to see Frieda standing there looking a little worried. 'Amelia, the police are downstairs and want you to accompany them to the police station. They won't tell me why, only that they want you to come straight away.'

'Tell them I will be down in five minutes,' said a puzzled Amelia. She quickly got dressed and met two very frightening-looking police with guns in holsters around the waists of their immaculate uniforms. They would give her no inkling what they wanted her for, and ordered her into their tiny Fiat police car. Amelia was by now feeling a little worried. Was it her passport? Had she misunderstood and needed a visa after all for this temporary work she was doing? Whatever it was she knew it would be sorted out once Franz knew about it.

She was shown into a room with a long, wide table with two chairs placed either side. A little old man with white hair, a wispy beard, spectacles and a friendly smile stood up and beckoned her to join him and patted the seat next to him. Opposite sat the Chief of Police and one of the men who had collected her. It was all terrifying but she started to relax when the little old man introduced

29

himself in cultured English as Professor Johann Stein, however her face took on a mask of incredulity when he explained what he was doing there and the charge against her. He explained that he had been called in to interpret to make sure she understood every word that was spoken as it was a serious charge. She could feel her heart pounding in her chest and her hands suddenly became clammy as she listened to the charge against her.

'Young lady. Were you at the Liftstuberl yesterday evening?' Feeling even more confused and frightened Amelia answered shakily, 'Yes'. The Professor then proceeded to tell her, 'It has come on good authority to the ears of the Chief of Police that you were drunk and dancing naked on the tables!'

Amelia was totally taken aback, then realising it must be an elaborate joke, laughed out loud. But her laughter quickly changed to fear when she saw the very strict, stern face of the Chief of Police. He banged his fist on the table. '*Ruhe!*' he commanded, his huge frame towering over her, the piercing steely blue eyes seemed like they bored into her very soul. She turned to the Professor and said incredulously, 'My God, you are being serious aren't you?'

'Yes indeed young lady, the source of this information is very reliable and I am afraid this a very serious charge,' he said with full conviction.

Amelia's fear was replaced with anger, justifiable anger. She stood up, faced the Chief of Police squarely and told him in excellent German that he had better check up on his so-called 'reliable source of information' as there was not a word of truth in it and if they had bothered to check this out with Annelies and Willi or the rest of the party who were at the Liftstuberl, they would find that this was an absolute load of rubbish! What sort of person would say such a wicked thing? The Chief of Police, now

30

looking a little flustered, told her to sit down and ordered the Professor and the other policeman to follow him out of the room.

Amelia sat there, her mind in turmoil. How could such a thing happen? There must be someone in the village who obviously bore her a grudge, but who and why? She more than got on well with everybody. Who could possibly hate her so much that they had to make up lies about her? It was frightening to think that someone wanted so desperately to discredit her. Sitting there with all these thoughts milling around in her head she suddenly felt extremely vulnerable – she was in a police station in a foreign country being charged with a serious offence. It didn't bear thinking about what her parents would say if they knew, but one thing was for certain, they would want her home straight away.

After half an hour, by which time she had sunk to the depths of despair, the trio returned. The Chief of Police looked very sheepish and was shaking his head. She could see he was acutely embarrassed as he mumbled an apology and left it to the Professor to explain what had happened. She had been the victim of a mischievous prank. Apparently Koni and a few of the others who had been at the Liftstuberl did not go home with the rest of the revellers but carried on drinking, ending up in the Hotel Post at breakfast time for coffee. Sitting at one of the tables in the smaller bar was Koni's arch-enemy Alfred, who was the brother-in-law to the Chief of Police. He was not a popular person and Koni loathed him because he was a snitch, so in a loud alcohol-fuelled voice Koni said to his equally inebriated friends, 'That was a great night, the best I've had for ages. The best part was when the drunken English girl peeled off her clothes and danced naked on the tables!' His friends, realising what he was up to, went along with it nodding and laughing. All of a sudden

Alfred shot off, straight to the police station and his brother-in-law.

The kindly Professor apologised on behalf of the police and assured her they would not go unpunished.

'Oh please, let's forget the whole matter, it was a very stupid prank and I was not amused. It was as much the fault of the police for not checking the story out instead of immediately bringing me to the police station in such an undignified manner. Now I just want to go back to the Rissbacherhof!'

Both men were told to apologise to Amelia, which they did. They were also told they must pay the fee of the Professor, which Koni flatly refused to do. He pointed out it was Alfred's fault for eavesdropping on a private conversation that was not meant to be taken seriously. Koni had a point so Alfred ended up having to pay the full amount. The story went around the village like wildfire and where there was contempt for Alfred there was sympathy for Amelia. As for Koni, he was well known for his practical jokes but never before taken seriously so his reputation was intact, whereas Alfred was even more unpopular. There was no doubt by the look of sheer delight on Koni's face how he had enjoyed getting Alfred into trouble.

Franz had arrived at the police station as soon as he heard about the debacle and was furious with the Chief of Police for pulling Amelia in without even checking on the story. He put his arm around Amelia's shoulders and led her to the tourist office where a concerned Heidi and Anna made her a coffee and told her like everyone else how enraged they were to hear what had happened.

'It's all over now and I just want to forget it,' said a subdued Amelia. Assuring them that she was all right and thanking them for their kindness she took her leave, pulled herself together and decided she was going back to the Rissbacherhof to have a shower, put some make-up on and go for a lovely walk up to the Alpenruhe.

Halfway up the mountain road a car approached from behind and stopped. Marcus jumped out and asked her where she was going. On hearing the Alpenruhe he said that was exactly where he was going too and invited her to jump in. 'I was appalled to hear what had happened to you Milli. It must have been a dreadful experience. I, and a few others, could bang their heads together for putting you through that. Are you okay now?'

Amelia nodded. 'It was like something out of a comedy sketch except it was very serious at the time, but if someone related this very story to me I would laugh, and if ever I have the nerve I shall tell my friends in England about it when we are in the pub one evening. You just can't make a story like this up!'

Marcus smiled and said Koni and Alfred could count themselves lucky that she was such a good sport because if she chose to she could get them into serious trouble.

'It's history Marcus, just another day of life in Bachl, but one I would not want to repeat.'

Changing the subject, Marcus went on to explain, 'I was sorry to miss the party but I had to finish this suit for Rudi as he wants it for a wedding he is going to in Schwaz on Saturday and I promised I would deliver it today.'

They were met by a grateful Rudi who invited them to stay to lunch. It never ceased to amaze Amelia the way she had been so readily accepted into this little community. She was so glad she was going to experience a ski season here – where she felt a great sense of belonging. The whole family came to greet them and it was obvious that they adored Marcus, they treated him like some sort of god. After lunch he asked her if she was in any hurry to get back to the village, to which she replied no but she had intended to go for a walk. 'I will join you Milli. Farther up the mountain there is one of the oldest farmhouses in Bachl, it's a nice walk.' She couldn't refuse such an offer especially as she had no fear of him, but now saw him in a different light and a very much respected member of the village. He was also extremely well read and funny, so all in all he was good company – as long as he didn't read anything into their relationship!

It took nearly an hour to reach the farmhouse where they were met by a delighted Peter, Maria and their eight children. They were poor farmers but contented and happy. They had cows, goats, pigs, chickens and a solitary horse that was used for ploughing. Marcus took her into the barn which was incorporated into the main house and entered from a door in the large hallway. The smell of animals was overwhelming but not in an offensive way. Marcus explained that the animals were kept inside in the winter but in the summer they were free to roam in the sloping fields behind the farmhouse. He said it was a wonderful sight to see when they were let out for the first time in the spring as they would slowly walk out of the barn and then start jumping in the air and running around madly.

They went and joined Peter and Maria in the enormous kitchen, which was also the living room. The children were fascinated by Amelia and urged her to talk more as they loved the English accent. After a very pleasant hour or so and several Schnapps it was time to make the descent. They were waved off by the whole lovely family who made Amelia promise to return. Marcus took her hand as they carefully traversed the exposed roots of the trees. It had been such an uplifting, unexpected experience she had all but forgot the despair she had felt earlier. As Marcus chatted away, she realised she owed a huge debt of gratitude to this man whom she had once – not so long ago – been trying to avoid. At Rudi's, Marcus picked up his car and drove Amelia back to the village. At the Rissbacherhof he planted a kiss on her cheek, thanked her for her company and drove off. Watching him leave she felt mixed emotions. She had no intention of becoming involved with anyone, it was far too soon after Alex, but there was no hiding the fact she was getting rather fond of Marcus.

The English lessons had been an enormous success and ended in mid-December when all the hotels and Gasthofs were open once again for the ski season. Everyone, especially the head of the ski school, was on tenterhooks as there had been only a few flurries of snow so far but it had been forecast for two days' time. The ground was ready after several days of heavy frost which meant when the snow finally arrived it would hold.

5

As promised, as the first guests arrived so did the snow. The heavens opened and it snowed and snowed and snowed, beautiful big fluffy flakes. The reps for the tour operators had arrived ten days in advance of their guests and Amelia got to know them all in a matter of days. The ski lifts were oiled up and raring to go after two days of continual snow that by then measured 32 inches in depth. The snow ploughs and piste machines were in constant use. The village looked so beautiful with the focal point being the huge Christmas tree festooned with fairy lights outside the church, and the church itself illuminated. There was great activity in the village and a great atmosphere.

Gretl soon taught Amelia the ropes which was just as well as the Konditorei was busy from the time it opened. Franz had helped her move her belongings into old Lois' house in the centre of the village where Gretl had prepared a room for her. Lois was a widower who lived alone in the big house. All his children were married and had their own homes, but he would not be budged from the place he had been brought up in. He had a little shoe shop on the ground floor where he did repairs and lived, which meant Amelia had the whole upstairs to herself, but she only needed her bedroom. Gretl had put up pretty curtains that matched the duvet, and a multi-coloured Tirolean carpet covered most of the floor in this all wooden-built house. A pair of lovely ornate wardrobes stood against one wall, they had beautiful religious scenes that had been hand painted by Lois' father, and a large chest of drawers to match. A wicker chair was placed in the corner and a table with a pretty lace cloth and a poinsettia stood under the window. Amelia loved it, it was so cosy – her little nest until the spring.

She soon fell into the routine of the Konditorei and was appreciated not only by Gretl and Georg but by the visitors too. The young girls on holiday all envied her as they themselves would have loved the opportunity to spend the whole ski season in Bachl. She would not have wanted to take up waitressing as a profession but was certainly going to enjoy the next three months or so. Her parents had not really been surprised at her announcement that she was staying the winter in Bachl but were happy that she was certainly over Alex. They looked forward to her letters that went into great detail about life in the village, which gave them some sort of insight into the little community their daughter had fallen in love with. This would be the first Christmas in 22 years that they would be without her so they had booked up for a Christmas and New Year in their favourite hotel in Scotland to make up for the absence of their beloved daughter. They both wondered how long it would be before she met someone who would really appreciate and love her as they did.

Amelia discovered the Tiroleans celebrated Christmas day on 24th December, when the families would gather together for a special dinner followed by carols around the tree and the opening of presents. At 11 pm they all headed to Midnight Mass. The church was packed, and loudspeakers were installed to relay the service to the crowd in the square outside. Afterwards, everyone poured into the square where the balcony of the Hotel Post was floodlit and members of the brass band were congregated. On the stroke of midnight they started to play 'Silent

Night'. Amelia, standing with the reps, felt a huge lump in her throat and could not contain the tears streaming down her face. As she fumbled for her tissue she noticed she was not the only one to be affected in this way – all the reps and others in the crowd were also dabbing at their eyes. It was so moving and beautiful, with people holding candles amidst a background of snow and huge icicles. It made Christmas what it was meant to be – a religious experience.

Jill the Thomsons rep was Amelia's favourite. The two just seemed to to hit it off, and Amelia had learned that Jill was there in the summer too and this was her fifth season. They had one great thing in common – their love of the village and its people. The locals had great respect for Jill as she looked after her guests properly, not like some of the reps who used their work as an excuse to have a prolonged ski holiday, and abused their position by spending too much time in the nightclubs and on the slopes instead of looking after their guests. A few had been sent home after Franz had complained to their company, and Jill seemed to be the Mother Hen who would remind them of their responsibilities and of what would happen if their company found out they were neglecting their duties. This was always a wake-up call to them.

After the service, Amelia was swept along with the reps for Gluhwein in the Post. This was another welcome new experience as she had never heard of this drink before but the delicious taste of the hot, mulled red wine flavoured with cinnamon, cloves, orange and lemon zest and sugar, was exactly what she needed for her chilled body. There was a great spirit of camaraderie between the locals and holidaymakers.

Marcus was surrounded by young girls in stunning ski outfits. He looked like he was enjoying it too. Jill, following

Amelia's gaze, told her that the girls fell head over heels in love with him and she could quite see why, he was such a handsome hunk but, like many of the instructors, fickle! Amelia could feel her colour rise as he walked towards them. Jill looked flabbergasted when he said, 'Hello Milli, Merry Christmas! And to you also Jill. Can I get you a Schnapps?' They both accepted and as he headed for the bar they were aware of the glares of the little band of girls he had left, and felt rather superior.

'You are a bit of a dark horse Amelia, I didn't realise you already knew him so well when I was mouthing off!' Amelia laughed and told her that she did not know him well but only as a friend and one of her pupils at the English classes. 'He certainly looked differently at you than me, and if I'm not mistaken he seems to have you on a bit of a pedestal,' said an amused Jill. Amelia told her that the last thing on her mind was an involvement again especially as it was so soon after her broken engagement. Jill was almost convinced until Marcus reappeared with the Schnapps and beer chasers and sat at their table. The girls were really glaring now. Jill was amused but Amelia was ashamed to admit to herself that she felt flattered. He stayed for a while making small talk but it did not go unnoticed that he obviously had a soft spot for Amelia. She, in return, remained calm and indifferent but Jill was not fooled.

Jill's flat was in a private house on the hill leading up to the village and she had to walk past Amelia's 'nest' to get home, so both feeling a bit light-headed they decided to call it a day. Arm in arm, stumbling and giggling, they tried to cope with the hidden, slippery, icy patches under the snow, as they made their way home. Marcus had returned to the girls, much to their delight, and left Amelia and Jill wondering which one, if any, would manage to single him out!

Christmas Day was the start of the ski school. The meeting place was on the nursery slope behind the church and where Toni Kogl, who was the head of the ski school, allocated the pupils their appropriate instructors. As the Konditorei was not opening until 10.30 that morning Amelia went along to see the spectacle and could hardly believe her eyes! Gone were the five o'clock shadows, scruffy hair, dirty fingernails and working clothes. Instead, in front of her was a transformed group of handsome, well-groomed men in sexy, smart ski uniforms of black ski pants topped by red jumpers and headbands with the ski school logo. They all acknowledged her and she felt so proud of them as they preened themselves in front of their groups. She stayed with the reps and watched the groups go off in various directions to their appropriate slopes. The ski school operated five days a week Monday to Friday, with individual members or small groups having the option of private lessons by the instructors at the weekends. This was very lucrative but after teaching all week it was usually only the unmarried men who volunteered.

At the Konditorei Amelia told Gretl of her surprise at seeing the transformation of the village men, and was told that their wives and girlfriends dreaded the ski season as the temptation that was put to them in the shape of starstruck girls – completely overwhelmed by the mountains, snow, their instructors and the whole romantic atmosphere – was something they had to put up with. It was their duty as instructors not only to teach but also to socialise with their groups. The men lapped up the attention but always returned to their wives and girlfriends. 'You will see what I mean when you experience the après ski sessions in the hotels and Gasthofs,' said Gretl looking lovingly at her husband who had never had aspirations to become an instructor and had never strayed. She was one of the lucky ones and well she knew it! Amelia knew that the womenfolk of the village were not emancipated and were expected to stay at home whilst their husbands and boyfriends were out all hours. 'That wouldn't do for me I'm afraid,' she replied seriously.

Franz had told her to go along to the ski hire shop and get fitted up for skis, boots and sticks, courtesy of the tourist office, in appreciation for the invaluable tuition she had given the instructors. So after work she trotted along to get kitted out. She had to wear the clumpy ski boots back to Lois' as she couldn't carry them as well as trying to balance the heavy skis on her shoulder. Walking on the snow and ice was no easy task in these boots and she was so glad when she finally reached the house.

Lois told her she could leave her skis and boots in the hall and asked if she was comfortable and satisfied with her accommodation, to which she replied yes, thank you, but didn't mention 'except for the loo!' Normally she did not stay too long in the house as she did not like the indignity of visiting the antiquated loo that was out on the balcony. It was the old wooden type and installed when the house had been built over 150 years ago. The seat had a hole in the middle and a big drop below. The worst thing was it was at the far end of her balcony and facing the Alpenhof hotel and ski school bureau. The Postbus and Skibus stopped at the busy square below, which was always milling with people. It meant that whenever she stepped out onto the balcony it was like stepping onto a stage. Worse still, anyone acquainted with these old houses would know exactly where she was going, especially as it was in a boarded structure with a little window carved out in the shape of a heart. When sitting on the loo one could admire the view but also her head could be seen from the street, so she had to sit in this pongy hole with her head down! She shuddered when

41

she thought of the first time she had had to use it. It was the early morning the day after she had moved in. It had snowed heavily during the night and as she had opened the balcony door she was met by a sea of faces below. She had quickly dropped onto her knees and crawled along to the loo. There was more than a foot of fresh soft snow on the balcony which meant her dressing gown and slippers were sodden – and then she had to crawl back again, freezing cold and wet. She vowed she would be making very few visits to the stinky bog if she could help it!

6

When she finished work the next day Amelia went and watched the beginners on the nursery slopes and, deciding it did not look too difficult, fetched her skis. The skis were not difficult to attach to the bindings but no one had told her that once the skis were fixed you had to edge them or you end up flat on your back – which was exactly what she did. The first thing that came into her mind was to look around and see if anyone had noticed, but the instructors and their groups were concentrating on their own skis. She struggled to her feet only to go straight down again. It was then she realised what was happening and managed to keep her balance and shuffled along for a few yards before giving up. Determined not to be put off she decided she would discreetly watch what the ski groups were doing the next day and then copy.

When she went to meet Jill at the Post for the après ski session she ran into Marcus in the hallway. 'The very person I wanted to see,' he said with a smile.

'Oh really, what can I do for you Marcus?' she replied.

'Well I heard about your attempt at skiing today and because you need lessons you can join my group as I have beginners this week.' Amelia's heart sank, as she thought no one had noticed her futile attempt. 'Don't be embarrassed *Millilein*. It's like everything else, all you need is a few basic lessons and you will be fine,' he assured her.

'That's very kind of you Marcus and yes, I will take you up on your offer.'

43

'Good! Good! See you tomorrow then for the afternoon class on the Postfeld.' He went off hurriedly into the bar.

She had an awful foreboding – it would have been much better to have had some lessons with one of the other instructors as she was terrified of making a fool of herself in front of Marcus. She was too aware of him as a friend rather than an instructor, but more to the point didn't want to make a fool of herself again. It was too late now and she couldn't get out of it. She told Jill about her day and her friend had agreed with Marcus, Amelia definitely should have lessons as it was impossible to pick skiing up without tuition. 'It will be great, Mel, because when you have learnt the basics I can take you out for practice sessions. It is the most wonderful feeling in the world – the freedom of swishing down the mountain in total control of your skis.'

Amelia felt a little more comfortable after talking to Jill but armed with skis, sticks, sunglasses and bumbag – complimenting her all-in-one ski suit – her confidence was slowly fading away when the next day she trudged in her heavy boots towards the nursery slopes a few minutes' walk away.

Marcus stood with his back to her chatting to his group. Her stomach did a flip, she wanted to turn and run but two things stopped her – her clumsy boots and Marcus having already seen her. He introduced her to the rest of the team as 'Milli'. Some of them already recognised her as the girl from the coffee bar and they seemed a friendly little crowd, which helped no end to relax her. 'Watch me, I will show you,' said Marcus as he proceeded to show them how to fix their skis onto their boots. 'One very important thing to remember is as soon as the skis are fixed you must edge them like this or they will start moving and you will fall over.' He looked mischievously at Amelia as he said this and she felt her colour rise. She pretended to be nonchalant, but didn't quite convince him.

'Now watch what I am doing and I want you to follow me in single file,' he said as he started to move slowly with the use of his sticks. It looked so easy and one by one they followed, except Amelia who was already wobbling, then fell over. Marcus side-stepped back to her and showed her how to get up, then explained she had not been watching carefully enough, as she had leaned back on her skis, with the instant result of falling over. 'Relax Milli, you will be okay I promise you,' he said gently. Aware of the rest of the team watching her she managed to do exactly as he showed her. Feeling very pleased with herself she was happy to note that she was the first to fall, but not the last, which restored her confidence a little!

Next, he went on to show them how to stop, by using the snowplough method. It was disastrous, she kept falling over and at one stage fell so awkwardly she knocked the rest of the group down like dominoes. Marcus was beginning to lose his patience a little which made Amelia ten times worse. She was trying so hard to please him but she was the worst one in the group. She felt she had let him down but was comforted by the fact the lesson was nearly over. Marcus came over to her and apologised for losing his patience a little. Noticing she was biting back tears of frustration he put his arm around her shoulder and told her not to worry as she would soon pick it up.

'No Marcus, I do not want to be in your class again, I will only hold you back. It will be a while before I even think of getting back on skis, but thank you for your help. I'm just sorry I let you down. Please do not try to talk me round, my mind is made up.'

Seeing it was futile to argue with her, he patted her shoulder and walked away.

45

7

Amelia loved her work, her little nest, the brilliant blue skies, snow, the après ski sessions, nightlife, in fact the whole concept of the ski season. While she was in this frame of mind Marcus joined her on the terrace. 'Milli, I am free tomorrow afternoon and I was wondering if you would like me to give you a private ski lesson as my thanks for the great improvement in my spoken English.'

'Your English was already very good, but thank you for the compliment and that is a very kind gesture.' Seeing the expectation on his face she couldn't be churlish, and quite surprised him by accepting his offer. He looked so relieved at not having another put-down, he just carried on and arranged where he would meet her the next day, then not pushing his luck took his leave and disappeared into the bar.

Sunday afternoon, as promised, he took her to the upper slopes with the drag-lift which at the first attempt she promptly fell off, but red-faced and determined she managed to accomplish her goal on the second. Not a good start! He looked so handsome and was so graceful on his skis. He made it look so easy but she was not an easy pupil. She tried so hard to follow his instructions but to no avail, she fell over again and again with the safety catch on her bindings continually opening. Marcus could see she was getting extremely frustrated and told her she was trying too hard, and to relax. She felt humiliated and was so angry at herself but she knew she would never be able to be taught by Marcus because she was now aware of him as being extremely attractive. Try as she might she could not ignore the fact that she was beginning to have feelings for him that she shouldn't have.

'Marcus I really do not want to carry on. Thank you for your time but it's obvious I am not a natural on skis despite your super instruction so I am now calling it a day,' she said as she sat in the snow with her head in her hands.

'You must persevere *Millilein*, if you give up now you will never get back on skis,' he said, hoping she would just get up and follow his instructions.

Rather than let him down she carried on, feeling bloody angry with herself for not being able to achieve what other beginners had, especially as she was having one to one instruction. She did improve but was so relieved when the two hours were up. 'Thank you Marcus, you have been so patient. I do feel I have benefited and I will persevere, but for now I would like to buy you a beer, as I don't know about you, I could certainly do with one or even two!'

They sat on the terrace of the Jagerhof with the locals, who had watched them approach with their skis and slyly gave each other knowing looks. Amelia had a chat with them, drank her beer, thanked Marcus again in front of all of them and casually made her exit.

After freshening up she was on her way out again, this time up to the Bergblick for her evening meal. Amelia had decided that as it was a good distance out of the village she was unlikely to meet any of the instructors – especially Marcus. The bar was packed with mostly members of the Queen's Own and the Royal Hussars regiments who came every year to Bachl for training before going on to St Moritz in February for the big ski races. Some of them were accompanied by their wives or girlfriends and recognised her from the Konditorei. They were very interested to know how she came to be in Bachl and fascinated by her story. They were good company and invited her to join them later at the Jagerkeller where they were heading to celebrate a birthday. It was good to be in such company, it was what she needed to put the thoughts of the disastrous afternoon and her feelings for Marcus behind her.

Franz was also at the Bergblick and was anxious to hear how she was getting on, so Amelia poured out the story of her diabolical attempt at skiing.

'Don't worry Amelia, I know just the person to teach you to ski. He was in your English class and lives at Innerbachl, where he can give you lessons away from the other instructors, especially Marcus. I will ring Julius and arrange some private lessons for you but please keep it to yourself,' he said seriously.

'What would I do without you dear Franz, you are such a darling,' said a very grateful Amelia who in a flash had her spirits lifted thanks to Franz Rissbacher.

'Come into the office on Tuesday and I will tell you the arrangements I have made. I can also promise you, Milli, that Julius is very easy going with lots of patience and I know you will be just fine.'

She entered the Jagerkeller with the army crowd, where Captain Michael Jones – 'call me Mike' – took her hand and led her onto the dance floor. Apart from being a lovely dancer he had a great sense of humour and was obviously very popular with the rest of his crowd. She was more on the dance floor than off and after several glasses of wine felt she had known them all her life! Glancing at her watch she noticed with a shock that it was 1.30 am and as she was working in the morning decided to call it a day, but Mike would not let her go without one last dance. He was holding her very close when there was a tap on his shoulder and on turning around he came face to face with Marcus.

'Excuse me, but I would like to dance with Milli,' Marcus said very politely.

Mike glanced at Amelia and said, 'You okay with that Amelia?'

'Thanks Mike, yes, this is one of my friends,' she said, trying hard not to be angry.

Marcus looked smug as he twirled her around the dance floor but was soon brought down by Amelia who let him know in no uncertain terms that she was with her friends and had not expected him to cut in on her dance. 'Sorry Milli,' said a tipsy Marcus, 'but he was holding you too close and I don't like him, he looks shifty!'

'How dare you assume the responsibility to choose my friends for me', she said angrily. 'What's more you have insulted a gentleman with your silly remarks and I will ask you not to assume I am a poor defenceless woman that you need to protect. Don't you ever, ever do such a thing again! Now go home and sleep it off.' With that she left, before Marcus had a chance to say anything else.

Walking home, Amelia went over and over the night's events. It was painfully obvious Marcus had been jealous and due to his tipsy condition let his feelings be known, and not only to Amelia. Whatever was I thinking of even allowing myself to have feelings for him, she thought, and promised herself she would give him a really wide berth after this little episode.

On Tuesday Franz told her that Julius was looking forward to teaching her and to meet him at Innerbachl after she finished work the next day. Julius proved to be just as patient as Franz had promised and after just one lesson, when Amelia had fallen over only once, she found her confidence had returned. After arranging with Julius for another lesson on Thursday a euphoric Amelia went

49

on to meet Jill at her office where they decided to go to the Post for their evening meal. While they ate Amelia confided to Jill what had happened the previous day.

'Forgive me for saying, Mel, but you made a big mistake in agreeing to a ski lesson with Marcus. What you in fact did was to raise his hopes but after putting him in his place at the Jagerkeller you might with any luck have dashed them! You are much better off sticking to the army crowd. They're a nice lot, I've known them ever since I first came to Bachl and you know if you ever need company you can always find me at my office during open hours.'

The talk at the Konditorei the next morning was all about the two Bavarians who despite being warned not to ski off-piste had gone ahead and caused an avalanche at Innerbachl. The village rescue service and a helicopter from Bavaria had circled the area until the light began to fail. They had continued the search at first light but it was impossible to locate them in the vast area of the avalanche. To make matters worse the snow had started falling thick and fast which made it more dangerous for the rescue services, so the search was called off. The bodies were not likely to be found until the spring when the snow would start to melt. Everyone was curious why a helicopter from Bavaria had arrived for the search, and the owner of the hotel where the victims had been staying answered their question. It was a government minister and his secretary who were missing. He should have been at a meeting in Munich, as his wife had been led to understand!

Sunday arrived and the heavy snow that had been falling the night before continued. The snowploughs and gritters were kept busy and the piste machines worked non-stop in readiness for the day's skiers.

Itching to get back on her skis with her new found

confidence, Amelia arrived at the drag-lift and with skis firmly on she donned her goggles underneath her bobble hat and slid onto the drag-lift. Perfect! Despite the falling snow, which had eased off a little, she skied gracefully right down to the start and felt on top of the world. Once back at the top she was joined by an open-mouthed Marcus. 'Well done *Millilein*, I didn't think you would ever make a skier but my goodness have you proved me wrong.'

'I had a good teacher,' she replied but could have eaten her words when she saw the surprise and hurt in his face. 'Sorry, what I really meant was I found it easier learning with someone else. Oh my God, that isn't what I meant either!' Finding herself digging a hole and falling in deeper she went on, 'I think I was too aware of you as a man and not a teacher to learn with you. Oh, what the hell! Please do not be offended as you are a superb instructor, it was not your fault that I was such a failure.'

Marcus just looked blank and then smiled, seeing how flustered she was getting. 'I will forgive you Milli if you come to the chairlift next Sunday. I will take you down the blue run. After watching you today you are ready for it. Your days on the drag-lift and nursery slopes are over.'

She surprised herself by accepting, and continued the morning going up and down the Jagerfeld until the snow started to fall heavier and heavier and she was getting fed up of continually scraping off the snow that was sticking to her skis in clumps. She found Marcus was giving a private lesson and that was why he was on the drag-lift and not the chairlift doing some serious skiing. She was quite pleased that he thought she was good enough to attempt the blue run and relished the thought of the chairlift and Wiedershorn mountain, especially as Julius was going to teach her parallel stops – then she really would feel like a skier! She couldn't wait to get out onto the piste straight after work every day and after two more lessons with Julius she had mastered parallel stops.

She went for her lunch at the Alpenhof and the first person she saw was Mike Jones who beckoned her to join his group at their table. The first thing he asked her was who was the tipsy man at the Keller the other night, to which she replied he had been one of her English class and quite harmless. 'He seemed very fond of you and quite possessive if you don't mind me saying,' remarked Mike.

Amelia found herself attempting to protect Marcus and passed it off as just a tipsy reaction. 'He's quite a nice person when he is sober and like the other pupils in my class he is just a good friend.' She changed the subject quickly by asking them what they had been up to. They were more interested in what she was going to do after the ski season was over. 'Much as I miss my parents and friends I really cannot bear to think of leaving Bachl and life will never be the same. My mother is due to go for a hip operation in April so I shall be helping my father run the hotel for the duration of the summer,' she explained.

They had all decided to call it a day unless the snow stopped, which meant they could return to the piste, and so two hours of interesting banter was quickly brought to a halt when the whole room lit up! The sun was shining and as they were headed back to the chairlift Mike asked Amelia if she would like to join them, but she declined as she wanted a bit more practice before attempting the blue run. 'In that case Amelia would you join me for dinner at the Bergblick this evening? They do the best Schnitzel in Bachl.'

'Thank you Mike, I would love to, about seven okay?' she replied without even thinking.

As she was walking back to continue her skiing on the

Jagerfeld she considered whether it had been wise to accept the dinner invitation, and then told herself Mike Jones was brilliant company, but perhaps she should not have allowed herself to be singled out. Too late now, she thought, and focused her attention on putting her skis on and getting back on the piste.

When it started to snow again she decided to go to the Krone bar. She noticed there were quite a lot of ski instructors there. Koni grabbed her and sat her down at the Stammtisch, a big table which was always reserved for the instructors. A beer was put in front of her and she was the subject of a lot of teasing when Johann, looking somewhat serious, asked her what drinking like a fish meant. Amelia could hardly keep a straight face and asked him where he had heard it, to which he replied he had asked a girl from his group out for a drink and she had replied, 'No thank you because I have heard you drink like a fish!' Amelia explained exactly what drinking like a fish meant and saw that instead of being insulted he was relieved that it didn't mean he drank with his mouth shaped like an O. If anything, he seemed to take it as a compliment!

The instructors always had many stories to tell of their ski groups. Amelia was sure some of it was pure fiction, just male bravado, but it provided endless amusement to the eagerly awaiting group. She had heard from a disgusted waitress that there was a kitty every week for whoever bedded the most holiday girls. Amelia was equally disgusted and, feeling brave and out of earshot of the others, she asked Marcus if this was true. He sheepishly replied that it was, and was quick to assure her he was no part of it. Hardly being able to grasp the implications of this distasteful practice but not quite believing, she asked him how they could prove their conquests and he replied, 'They can't, the kitty is based purely on trust. No one apart from the instructors are supposed to know this Milli, so I advise you to forget about it. It is not meant to harm anyone and it would give the instructors a bad name.'

'Marcus, I would be ashamed to repeat what I have just heard, and you are right it wouldn't exactly enhance the reputation of the instructors, but I must say it is an unsavoury way of trying to prove their masculinity.'

After returning home to freshen up and get changed, Amelia met Mike at the Bergblick, where they had a delicious meal. It was a relief to find he had invited her for dinner purely because he enjoyed her company and had no ulterior motives. She was just a little annoyed with herself that she kept on looking around whilst having dinner in case Marcus appeared. She couldn't put her finger on why but the thought unnerved her. As it turned out, he was nowhere in sight. Dinner over, they joined the other Hussars for a memorable evening of talking, dancing and much laughter.

8

By the time the following Sunday arrived Amelia had enjoyed her skiing so much she was really looking forward to the challenge of the blue run. As arranged the week before, she met Marcus at the Liftstuberl and joined the queue of weekend skiers. There were many from Bavaria due to its close proximity to the Tirol. She sat in wonderment as she ascended the Wiedershorn. Underneath, the skiers were traversing the slopes, and the only sounds were the swish, swish, swish of the skis. The village looked like it was miles away and every chair was occupied going up but the ones coming down were empty except for a few non-skiers who had ascended only for the fabulous views from the top. Once there, she was reminded of the day – which seemed an eternity ago – when Marcus had taken her right up to the top of the Rossberg after the Liftstuberl incident. She realised then that out of the three mountains surrounding Bachl she had witnessed the breathtaking views from the pinnacle of two with Marcus. It was heady stuff.

Marcus pointed out the blue run which snaked through the trees, hit a clearing and then more trees and another clearing before coming in sight of the lift station and the last lap. He told her normally it would take about seven minutes for experienced skiers but obviously it would take much longer than that for her first descent. With that he shot off with Amelia following, stopping at the entrance through the trees. 'Be careful here Milli as this will be bumpy so keep your knees flexible,' he warned her. He was right, it was bumpy and the first one she hit she lurched forward, with her bindings opening immediately on impact and her skis falling off before she hit the ground. He side-stepped back and helped her into the skis, then waited until she regained her balance before setting off again. This time, thought Amelia, I am not going to even try to keep up with him, I shall concentrate on these bumps. Even so she went over again and again. Marcus was extremely patient, so he thought, but she stretched his patience to within a whisper of him losing his cool when she was just not doing as he instructed.

'Marcus, you are unnerving me so please go ahead and leave me to it and I will meet you at the lift station,' she said very firmly and was surprised when he agreed. With a swish of his skis he had disappeared through the trees. Good! Now I can get on with it and not worry about holding him back she said to herself. Several other skiers passed her and, try as she might, she went over on nearly all the bumps she encountered. By the time she arrived at the first clearing she was aware twenty-five minutes had passed. The clearing was pure bliss, which she happily skied over in a matter of minutes until the trees loomed dark and menacingly ahead.

She was by now dying to go for a wee but knew she would have to wait until she got to the bottom. She could have kicked herself for having that hot chocolate just before she had met Marcus but too late to think of that now! With that thought in mind she slowly snowploughed into the narrow path through the trees. Some of the bumps she managed but others which had sneakily appeared and for which she was not ready found her bindings opening again and again. By now she was absolutely desperate to go to the loo and with a sigh of relief she saw the clearing and last lap ahead.

She skied effortlessly down to the ski station and frantically took off her skis and belted for the loo. Oh no! There was a long queue that snaked around the building. The feeling of relief at being down and near the loo had relaxed her muscles and thinking quickly she sat on a mound of snow, and felt warm then cold as she realised she had peed herself. Horrified, she heard her name called. It was Marcus, he was shouting at her not to sit on the snow or she would have wet trousers. A faint smile overtook the horror of what had happened as she realised Marcus had inadvertently handed her an excuse on a plate as to why her trousers were wet. By the time he got to her she apologised and made the excuse that she just did not think, and oh dear her trousers were wet. 'I just wanted to sit down after that lengthy marathon down the mountain and I am sorry if I have let you down but I did my best and it is obvious I'm not good enough to tackle the blue run yet,' she said, her bottom already beginning to feel icy cold.

'Come inside and have a hot chocolate and forget about the blue run. There's plenty of time for you to practise the bumpy patches,' he said softly. She declined, as all she wanted to do was get home and change out of her sodden trousers. Fortunately the ski bus was standing room only so she had no problem getting back to the village.

When she met Jill later she swore her to secrecy before embarking on the story of her disastrous afternoon. Jill tried to keep a straight face but couldn't hold it back and went into convulsions of laughter, to which Amelia found herself joining in. 'How about coming on the Innsbruck and Italy trip on Friday Mel, it will keep you out of mischief and also be good for you to get out of the village for a day, apart from the fact that I shall enjoy your company,' said Jill earnestly.

'Okay, I will ask Gretl if I can change my day off, and you're right, it would be good to get out of the village for the day, not to mention being able to visit Innsbruck and Sterzing. Thanks Jill!'

After arranging with Gretl the swap-over of her day off Amelia happily carried on with her work. She was glad to see Julius arrive with his wife for one of their regular visits for hot chocolate and gateaux. When there was a quiet moment she joined them, and in answer to his query about her skiing she related the problem she had in tackling the blue run. 'There is a slope in Innerbachl full of bumps where you can have a good practice Milli, let me know when you can make it and I will show you exactly how you can master them, no problem!' he offered. Amelia jumped at the chance, and told his wife Mariedl what a lovely husband she had and how lucky she was. Mariedl said lovingly, 'I know.'

Amelia had a wonderful day with Jill at Sterzing/Vipitano and Innsbruck and loved the interesting commentary Jill expertly gave along the way. At Innsbruck whilst having a coffee in the palace garden restaurant Amelia remarked how she would love to be a rep. Jill told her that with her rapport with people, her enthusiasm and her knowledge of the German language she would be in the front line if she approached a travel company. She also suggested Amelia spoke to Franz Rissbacher as he knew all the reps' managers in the Tirol and would certainly give her a good reference. Amelia absorbed all this and listened to Jill's advice about getting the ball rolling as soon as possible as the managers were about to start interviewing reps for the next season – also the existing reps had preference and could choose which resort they wanted.

On their return to Bachl, and after thanking Jill for such an enjoyable day, Amelia went back to the Konditorei and thought very carefully about taking the next step.

The more she thought about it the more it made sense and the next morning found her at the tourist office. Franz listened with interest what she had to say and agreed it was a very good idea. He would get straight on to Anne-Marie, the British Airways Manager in the Tirol. 'I will get in touch with you as soon as I have had a reply,' he said eagerly.

Amelia left the office with wings on her feet. It was only a few hours later that Franz arrived at the Konditorei to tell her that Anne-Marie would be in Bachl on the 28th of the month to interview her. Amelia was over the moon!

True to her word Anne-Marie arrived and after talking to Amelia for half hour realised she had found a rep for Bachl for the following winter. Franz had given a glowing report and on meeting Amelia, she could see why. 'I would like you to come to my office in Seefeld at the end of February to cover all the formalities and also meet all the other reps who will be working in the Tirol next winter,' she said, feeling very pleased to have another first class rep aboard. Amelia could hardly wait to tell Franz and Jill.

The cold January days unfolded into warm February ones. It would be difficult to explain to anyone who had not experienced this that, apart from the best skiing conditions of the season, the sunshine-filled days were hot enough to ski in T-shirts or blouses, unless it was actually snowing. The hotels and Gasthofs were packed to capacity for this, the carnival month. The main carnival day was the most important of the month when the locals, adults and children alike, really threw themselves into the fun-filled day and donned breathtaking costumes, and imaginative props went on parade. Girls from the village brass band served Schnapps from little barrels that were attached to their waists with a belt. There were German sausage and Schnapps and beer stalls dotted around the centre of the village. The brass band played waltzes, marches and folk music continuously, with the culmination of the day being the ski instructor event on the Jagerfeld. These fun-loving men skied from top to bottom of the steep slope dressed in the most outrageous costumes and with even more outrageous props, to the delight of the huge watching crowd of inspired, astonished holidaymakers. Gorillas, clowns, priests, big-bosomed women, babies with nappies sucking on oversized dummies, pantomime cows and horses, Chinese dragons and many, many others! The penultimate were a pair in an old oblong tin bath using ski sticks to steer themselves as they traversed the slopes. The crowds were in wonderment and even more so when the highlight and last to appear was Gottfried on six-foot stilts. To the deafening cheers, clapping and whistling of the crowds he traversed from top to bottom. As each instructor had neared the finishing line they had to ski through an igloo that housed a bar and were handed Schnapps as they skied through the entrance and out the exit without stopping – all except Gotts on his stilts!

For the villagers and holidaymakers alike it was a magical day with everyone feeling euphoric and not wanting the day to end. Afterwards, Amelia joined Marcus, Johann, Koni, Hermann, Willi and Sepp at a table near the bar at the Jagerhof where Koni, the ever-practical joker, said, 'Watch this.' He opened his packet of cigarettes and left one prominently sticking out and placed it on the table. Fuzzi, all five foot of him, drunkenly weaved and stumbled to their table and true to form helped himself to a cigarette. Standing there swaying as he tried several times to light it he finally succeeded as everyone at the table watched, not knowing quite what to expect. Suddenly there was an almighty bang as the cigarette, its end shredded, hung from his mouth. He had nearly jumped out of his skin and when a few seconds later he regained his composure, a hopping-mad Fuzzi chased a manically laughing Koni out of the hotel threatening to kill all six foot of him! The rest including Amelia were doubled up with laughter.

The day finally ended up at the Keller in the early hours with revellers going straight into breakfast afterwards. Amelia danced many times with Marcus but declined when he offered to take her home. She had not stayed too late and with her work the next day foremost in her mind she left while the party was in full swing. Going over the unforgettable day she had just experienced she gave a deep sigh and promptly dropped off into a deep, happy sleep.

9

Amelia awoke early to a pain in her right side and quickly realised it was the grumbling appendix that had not bothered her for some time. She had suffered from this complaint for several years and had found that the pain went away as quickly as it started. The trouble was she never knew when it was going to flare up. She went off to work hoping it would go away soon but instead of easing off it began to get worse.

Gretl noticed she was not her usual bubbly, chatty self and at a closer look saw the pain etched in Amelia's face. Concerned, Gretl asked her what was wrong and was told it was a grumble and normally passed after a few hours. Gretl insisted she went up to their sitting room to rest, and was not to come down until she felt better. Despite Amelia's protests Gretl ushered her upstairs. It was a very busy day at the Konditorei but Gretl assured her that customers didn't mind waiting for a few minutes. Amelia was glad to lie down with a hot water bottle but found that was not giving her any comfort. It was now really hurting instead of just a dull pain. She was beginning to feel sick when Gretl arrived with a camomile tea and nearly dropped the cup when she took one look at Amelia's face. It was chalk white and her lips appeared blue. She immediately phoned the doctor and when he heard the symptoms he left a surgery full of people and hurried across to the Konditorei. His suspicions were confirmed as soon as he examined her. It was appendicitis!

'We have got to get her to Schwaz hospital right away. There is no time to get an ambulance up but I noticed there are some of the British army in the café, I will go and ask their help,' he said as he rushed from the room.

The four 11th Hussars gently carried her to their Mercedes, propped her up on the back seat and surrounded her with cushions. They manoeuvred the twists and bends of the mountain road in record time and once in the valley were on the Autobahn. It took barely 40 minutes from the time they had left the village to the steps of the hospital where the stretcher was waiting to whisk her into theatre. Amelia was by now almost unconscious from the excruciating pain. The Hussars waited until she was in recovery before returning to Bachl. The surgeon phoned Ernst the doctor to give a progress report and divulged that if it had not been for his and the Hussars' prompt action Amelia could have died, as the appendicitis was turning into peritonitis. As it was, Amelia had a bigger than normal scar and was very sore, but the surgery had been successful and she would be in hospital for 10 days but was not allowed visitors for 24 hours.

When Amelia came to, she was aware of feeling groggy and very sore. Her first sight was of a lady in a white starched hat standing by her bed holding her hand. The lady turned out to be the matron who spoke to her in English and in comforting tones. Amelia kept drifting in and out of consciousness due to the painkillers and at some stage sank into a deep sleep. She awoke to the sound of a baby crying. 'Where the hell am I?' she thought. At the same time a sharp pain shot through her body as she tried to straighten her legs. She brought her knees back up, which eased the pain, and then slowly looked around the room. There, in the next bed, and the next, and also the three beds opposite were mums and their newborn babies. Just as she was thinking she was hallucinating the matron approached.

'How are you feeling Milli?' she asked.

Before Amelia could reply the matron apologised for her being brought into maternity, but after her operation there had been no room for her in the women's surgical ward and this had been the next best thing. A private room was now ready for her and she would be moved after lunch.

The next day in between bouts of dozing she could hear yodelling in the distance which seemed to be getting nearer by the minute, until her door burst open and in streamed nine instructors, led by Marcus. They all carried tall, brown, supermarket bags filled to the brim with chocolates, biscuits, wine, magazines and the inevitable Schnapps. She was completely overwhelmed and so touched to hear how worried they had all been. Marcus grabbed the seat nearest her bed, while some of the others plonked themselves on the bed itself. Amelia let out a stifled scream, as even the slightest movement was extremely painful. They quickly jumped up saying, 'Sorry, sorry, sorry.' It was then that she noticed Marcus was holding her hand. He told her of the shock they all had when it had spread around the village that it was a life or death situation. The 11th Hussars had become heroes, as the story had unfolded that if it had not been for their speedy action it would have been a completely different scenario, and it was fortunate that some of the army were still in Bachl as most of the regiment were already in St Moritz. The instructors were all very eager to see her scar, but no way was she going to satisfy their curiosity and, as if on cue, the sister arrived and ushered them all out as visiting time was over. They all gave her a peck on the cheek with Marcus being the last.

'Get well soon *Millilein*, we miss you in the village.

Gretl said to tell you not to worry about work as she has got one of the village girls to stand in for you until you are strong enough to return.'

'Tell her I can't wait to get back, the doctor said I was going to be in for at least ten days and afterwards at least a week's rest.' She didn't mention that the doctor had also said no lifting for six weeks, but with the agony she was in every time she moved or coughed there was nothing further from her mind.

After ten days Amelia was pronounced fit to leave but with a warning to take it easy. They must be joking, Amelia thought as she slowly walked, with every step making her wince, there is no way I could do anything else! She was happy when the sister told her that someone was on his way from Bachl to collect her. She gathered her belongings and went downstairs to wait in reception. Large as life, Marcus strode through the double doors, picked up her bag and offered his arm to support her.

'This is very kind of you Marcus,' she said leaning heavily on his arm. She felt so annoyed and embarrassed with herself that she could only shuffle along. Marcus was treating her like cotton wool and told her not to worry as they had all the time in the world and it was better to be slow and sure, not that she had any choice! She dozed most of the way back to the village where Marcus took her straight to the Konditorei on instructions from Gretl who had converted the ground-floor office into a comfortable makeshift bedroom/sitting room for her until she was well enough to return to her nest. It was such a welcoming sight. There was a constant stream of visitors, which made her feel very humble. What lovely caring people these are, they have made me feel like I am one of them, she thought, and indeed she was.

During her time spent recuperating Amelia made several visits to the reps' meetings which were usually at the

Jagerhof for coffee. She had come to know them all very well but her overall favourite was Jill. The reps were from Thompsons, Inghams, Blue Sky, Enterprise and Crystal. She learned such a lot by just listening to them, and felt more and more enthusiastic about the coming winter season. After nearly two weeks' rest she felt well and able enough to return to her nest and to start work again, but somewhat slower.

10

The Winter Dance was held every year in the Post hotel and was mainly for the locals. It was an opportunity for the wives and girlfriends to get together and an excuse to don their glad rags. In their dirndls they were a picture to behold. It was such a flattering costume – a pinafore dress, the bodice laced up at the front, nipped in at the waist and full skirted with an apron that matched. Under the bodice little white blouses with puffed sleeves were worn. Their outfits were completed with patent or suede shoes with a buckle at the front. The older women had matching hairstyles – a traditional Tirolean farmhouse plait that encircled their heads like a halo. The women were complemented by their menfolk in their Tirolean grey woollen suits with green lapels and matching buttons. Some had a little sprig of silk flowers – alpenrose, edelweiss or gentian – in their top buttonhole. Amelia had accumulated three dirndls, two for her work at the Konditorei and one for best.

She visited the hairdressers in the afternoon and emerged a while later with her hair piled on top of her head in a chignon dotted with little pink silk roses. Dressed in her stunning pale blue and pink dirndl she hardly recognised herself! She was still a little sore from her scar so restricted herself to waltzes only. In contrast to the dances she had been to in England where the men were often reluctant to get on the dance floor, the Austrian men loved their dancing and would be on the floor for every dance –

except when they were at the bar. Amelia was sitting at a big table with her Austrian friends, chatting away and catching up on all the local gossip, when Marcus appeared and asked her to dance. Holding her close as they danced he remarked upon how lovely she looked and if he didn't know differently he would be convinced she was a Tirolean girl. Accepting the compliment gracefully she stopped herself from telling him that apart from being a beautiful dancer and charming, she could quite understand how girls fell head over heels for him. Instead, she let herself be gently waltzed around the room. He was very attentive and when the dance finished led her back to her seat and pulled up a seat next to her.

They were aware that some English girls had entered the room and gone straight to the bar. The wives and girlfriends looked on suspiciously, especially as they appeared to be tipsy. The girls looked around the room and as soon as they recognised their instructors made a beeline for them. The instructors had to dance with them when asked, but were followed by the stony glares of their womenfolk. 'Can't they be asked to leave?' Amelia asked Marcus, to which he replied, 'No, even though the dance is not advertised some always find their way here and there is nothing we can do about it.' Amelia cringed to see these girls making fools of themselves and felt embarrassed that they were her own countryfolk.

One slip of a thing approached their table and holding her hand out to Marcus said, 'Marki darling, come and dance with me.' Seeing him look at Amelia she continued with, 'I'm more exciting than that frump by your side,' obviously assuming that Amelia was Tirolean and therefore did not understand English. Amelia stood up, looked the girl straight in the eye and said, 'That's debatable, and this frump understands English. Now bugger off you little tart and go and annoy someone else.' The girl looked as if she had been slapped, and with a red face went back to her friends. They all glared at Amelia and left.

The Austrian women wanted to know what she had said and were told by their amused husbands and boyfriends. Amelia had made friends for life in the village women! Marcus was not so amused. 'She is part of my ski group Milli and has been flirting all week not just with me. You should have ignored her.'

'I beg your pardon but I have never let anyone insult me before and I don't intend to start now. She was way out of order but she will think twice in future before assuming that anyone wearing a dirndl does not understand English!'

Johann came over and asked her for a dance before they could continue the conversation. Amelia now felt angry with Marcus as well as that ignorant girl. Damn it, she thought, I am not going to let anyone spoil my evening. Then she put the incident out of her mind to enjoy the rest of the night. Marcus had got up and left shortly after she had gone onto the dance floor.

A few days later at the Konditorei a tall, attractive Italian-looking man ordered a coffee and on hearing her accent asked what part of the UK she was from. When she replied, 'The West Country,' his ears picked up and he continued with, "I was at Exeter University for two years, they were two of the most unforgettable years of my life.'

'Exeter is where I live. How long ago were you there?' she asked.

'It must be about ten years ago now, but I remember it vividly and promised myself I would get back one day and visit my old friends, but there never seems to be time these days,' he said looking pensive.

'You certainly have not lost your command of English, it is an unmistakable, cultured, university accent,' she told him earnestly.

'Thank you for the compliment. Do you have a name?' he asked.

'It's Amelia, but I am known in the village as Milli. Oh would you please excuse me, there is someone waiting to order, nice to have met you.'

'Likewise', he answered.

The café got very busy then and she never even noticed him leave.

Later on that afternoon she was in the Jagerhof waiting for Jill when from behind her a voice said, 'Hello again Milli' and turning, she saw the same man smiling at her. 'I didn't have a chance to introduce myself earlier, my name is Lucien – Luc for short,' he said holding out his hand.

'Hello, Luc for short', she laughingly answered.

He asked her if she didn't mind him joining her, to which she nodded and beckoned to an empty seat at her table. 'I'm waiting for my friend Jill who is a rep but please take a seat.'

He started the conversation by saying how delighted he was to meet someone from Exeter and chatted about what he used to get up to in his student days in the city. She learned he had taken over the family business in Innsbruck upon the untimely death of his father eight years before. He came up to Bachl regularly for the weekend as a means of unwinding. It was his favourite place and only an hour's drive from his home. He was fascinated to hear about how Amelia came to be there and told her if ever she was in Innsbruck to give him a ring and he would personally give her a guided tour of his beloved city. With that he handed her his business card, just as Jill approached.

The look on Jill's face was a picture as Amelia introduced her new friend. Luc excused himself as he had promised to meet friends and was gone, leaving a gaping Jill following him with her eyes.

'Where on earth did you find such a hunk Mel? He's absolutely gorgeous!' When Amelia told her she said, 'I think perhaps I'm in the wrong job after all!'

'You might not believe this Jill but he didn't have that effect on me, I just thought he was nice to talk to especially as we have Exeter in common.'

'Do you know, Mel, I don't honestly think you have any idea how attractive you are to men. For someone so pretty and with a great sense of humour you have very low self esteem,' said Jill earnestly.

'It's because of what happened in Exeter I suppose. It's going to take time for me to learn to trust again but that is not going to stop me from admiring the male species. My motto now is Look But Don't Touch!' answered Amelia with a grin.

Anne-Marie had phoned Franz to say she had to come up to Bachl on business and would like to see Amelia if he could organise it. On hearing this Amelia arranged to meet her at the tourist office at the end of the week, hoping she had not changed her mind. 'On the contrary Amelia, I have brought all the necessary documents with me to engage you as rep for Bachl for next winter to save you the trip up to Seefeld,' she told her. After all the formalities were over, Amelia was armed with her contract and instructions about the seminar in Seefeld the following December.

'It's a four-day seminar where you will meet all the other reps and learn the ropes. You'll be staying at a very nice hotel there and will enjoy the experience, even though it is demanding with a lot to cram in. I have no doubts whatsoever you will sail through it and make a very good rep,' said Anne-Marie. 'What you must do is organise your accommodation for the winter, preferably somewhere with access to a phone in case of emergencies. The company will pay for this accommodation within reason and we have found that an apartment in a Gasthof is usually the best bet. If you try one of the Gasthofs we use first, you might be in luck, otherwise make sure it is somewhere easily accessible to the village.'

Feeling light-headed Amelia left the interview with a spring in her step. She could hardly wait to tell Jill, and decided to kill time by going to the Alpenhof and having a look at the reps' 'Guest Information' book. She sat in the bar and read it from cover to cover and was amazed by the amount of work that went into it. God! This must have taken ages to put together. There was detailed information including photos of every day excursion and evening entertainment. There was also a wealth of useful tips and hints. There had to be one book for each establishment the company used, in Jill's case seven. There was a big notice on the front of the book: 'Please do not take this book from reception as it is being constantly used'. Amelia thought it would be a very good idea to come back to Bachl in mid-November to enable herself to get acquainted with the procedures and make notes. The information books had to be done in one's own individual style and although you could get ideas from other reps' books you were not expected to copy.

Jill was delighted and promised to help in any way she could. She suggested Amelia went to Georg's travel bureau and get leaflets for the winter excursions they were expected to take, and upon hearing her plan to return in November suggested she made day trips out to these places to glean as much of the local history of the area as possible. The commentary on trips out was very important to the guests as they loved to hear about the folklore and customs of the places they visited – with some funny stories thrown in! Jill said that several of the reps did the minimum of research and copied almost word for word what the other reps had written, giving very little detail, which did not endear them to the guests who compared their information to the other tour operator books at the hotels. These were the girls who made bad reps as they obviously did not take their work seriously and saw the job as one long skiing and night-clubbing holiday, not caring for their guests as expected. Jill went on to tell Amelia that when it came to the attention of the tourist office that these girls were neglecting their duties, their managers were sent for and the girls were issued with a stern warning and very often sent home.

Amelia smiled wistfully and said, 'Do you know, Jill, I feel I have found my niche in life, it feels so right. My life must have been extremely boring before but I never recognised it as such until I had something to compare it with. My broken engagement was the best thing that ever happened to me, although I didn't realise it at the time. Do you know, I never even think about it now,'

'You will make an excellent rep Mel, and I look forward to working with you so much,' replied Jill, obviously very happily thinking about the next winter in Bachl.

When she returned to her nest, Amelia found a letter waiting for her from her mother who wrote how much they were all looking forward to seeing her soon. When she finished reading the letter, Amelia had a strong desire to have a hug from her Mum again. There was a special closeness between Eileen and her daughter, they had never once had a cross word. She could read Amelia's thoughts and there was no pulling the wool over her eyes when something was bothering or upsetting her. It had been the same ever since she was a little girl. Amelia knew she had a mum in a million. Her father was of a strong character, a perfectionist and a little Victorian in his ways. He would make his opinions known whether you wanted to hear them or not. He only wanted the best for his daughter, which wasn't always necessarily the same as what she wanted. This frequently led to clashes – both being as strong-willed as the other. Eileen was the calming influence in the family.

Amelia asked Gretl the next day when she was supposed to finish and was told that it would be the twenty-eighth of March as that is when the tour operators finished, but the Konditorei would stay open for the locals and weekenders until Easter. That afternoon Amelia wrote back to her mother, letting her know when she would be returning to the UK.

11

The weeks passed quickly, too quickly. The snow was leaving the sunny side of the village, but there was still plenty on the shaded side. It seemed that armies of yellow, white and blue crocuses appeared overnight on the banks and in the green fields on the sunny side, whereas there was still snow and skiing on the opposite mountain. Because it was getting quieter in the Konditorei Amelia had more time to talk to Luc when he next appeared. They talked a lot about Exeter and somehow Amelia sneaked into the conversation that she was coming back for the winter season, but as a rep.

"That's good news, Milli,' he said, but before she had chance to give him any details the café started to get busy again. 'Would you join me for dinner this evening at my hotel Milli, as I would love to hear more about your new venture?' he asked. Without even thinking she replied that she would love to, and agreed to meet him at the Alpenhof at six-thirty. She had quite surprised herself as her normal reaction would have been to decline, but he was such charming company and it seemed like she had known him for ages.

The restaurant in this rustic hotel was beautifully furnished in typical Tirolean style with masses of silk flowers on the tables and in huge vases around the wood-panelled dining room. Crisp, spotless, pink cotton cloths covered each table, with matching napkins folded artfully to resemble water lilies at each setting. They were shown to a corner table and no sooner had they arrived than the waiter appeared with a bottle of bubbly. While he was pouring it Amelia glanced around the room. Why am I doing this, she thought. The truth was she did not want to upset Marcus, as he seemed to have taken over as her protector. She was aware he had strong feelings for her but whereas she enjoyed his company in small doses she knew she could not cope with an involvement, so kept him at bay. He is not likely to be in this restaurant anyway, she reckoned, putting any more thoughts of Marcus on one side and looking forward to her evening with Luc.

When the menu was brought she told Luc he could order for her, as she just loved everything. 'Well in that case I shall order my favourite and hope it will be yours too,' he said. When the starters arrived it was an oval dish with some sort of meat in a garlic buttery sauce. 'This smells appetising,' she said as she broke off a chunk of bread and dipped it into the sauce. It was delicious but she could not recognise what sort of meat it was. Luc seemed surprised that she had never had it before and tried not to smile when he saw the look on her face when he said *escargots*. She bravely ate it all and remarked that it had been a new experience, reasoning with herself it was only meat, same as lamb or beef, pork or liver or kidneys. But it wasn't, it was snails. Those slimy things with little horns on their heads. Luc filled her glass up and pretended not to notice how quiet she had become!

The trout and almonds arrived and she found she was getting her appetite back and tucked in, chewing this time and not swallowing whole as she had done with the snails! The empty champagne bottle had long been replaced with her favourite white Italian wine, which by the time the dessert arrived was also empty. They had chatted away like old friends right through the meal and when asked if she would like cheese and biscuits a light-headed Amelia said, 'Oh no thank you Luc, another crust and I will bust!' This really tickled him, and when over their coffee and liqueurs she told him the story of the elderly road sweeper who had worked on the Exeter council for sixty years before retiring and when interviewed by a reporter from the local newspaper declared that he had been using the same sweeping brush for sixty years, and in all that time had only had three new heads and two new handles, Luc was in hysterics with Amelia joining in. They left the table and went into the bar for a nightcap, not that either needed one. Luc was still laughing and Amelia had a tipsy smile on her face. There were several locals there who witnessed this happy couple, put two and two together and made five – this was a juicy bit of gossip! It had been a really lovely evening and Amelia told him so – more than once. When they eventually left, Luc, like the gentleman he was, made sure she got home safely and said he would be up the following weekend and hoped she would join him for dinner again. Yes, that would be lovely thanks, she replied as she tried to get the key in the door and then promptly fell over the step.

True to his word, Luc arrived back the following weekend, which was Amelia's last before returning mid-week to England. She enthusiastically told him of how she looked forward to becoming a rep and how she was coming out in the last week in November to do some preparation in readiness for the seminar in Seefeld. His ears pricked up at this. 'I have a summer house in Seefeld,' he said. 'Just let me know when you will be there and I will show you the sights.' To which she replied that she did not think there would be much time for anything else other than the seminar if what she heard was true. It was a very intense course with a lot to cover but if she did have time then she most certainly would give him a ring. She told him how lucky she was to have found a cosy modern apartment in a new house which was only a six or seven minute walk from the village and which she could have all winter.

'Perhaps then when you come out in November you will give me a call, and I will give you a guided tour of Innsbruck,' he said hopefully.

'I would love that and will hold you to it Luc. I will also send you a postcard from Exeter to remind you of your student days.'

Sitting in the bar chatting away to Luc she did not see the pained expression on Marcus's face when the friends with whom he was playing cards at a corner table pointed them out. So it is true, he thought, she has got a boyfriend, and carried on playing cards as if he wasn't bothered. But he was! He had seen little of her since the dance as he had been busy trying to combine his ski instructing with his orders for suits that were needed for Easter. It was ironic that of all the girls he could have, the very one he wanted didn't want to know. This was a new experience and not one that he enjoyed or knew how to cope with.

All packed up and ready to go, and already having said her goodbyes, Amelia sat in the taxi with Georg and was a bit hurt that Marcus had deliberately avoided seeing her to say goodbye. She instinctively looked up to his workshop window and saw him standing there; he gave her a slight wave and was gone. The taxi pulled away, with Jill and the other reps waving her off. Even though she was looking forward to seeing her parents she felt it a great wrench leaving her beloved Bachl and by the time the taxi reached the station her spirits were down in her boots. Georg waved until the train was nearly out of sight and Amelia felt a strange compulsion to jump off again.

She had a rapturous welcome from her parents. Eileen and Charles noticed first of all her bronzed beautiful face and then that the confidence and self-esteem, which had been knocked out of her at her broken engagement, had returned with a vengeance. She was positively glowing and they soon found out why, when she told them of her plans for the following winter. It was a bit of a shock at first but they soon came around to the idea when they heard the details. She had omitted to tell them about her appendicitis, she was going to wait for the right moment and then play it down. It had not taken her long to realise her mother was in great pain and her heart went out to her. It would be such a relief to get this wretched operation over and to see her walking without limping and without pain.

The family hotel was fully booked from May until September so Amelia knew she was going to have her work cut out which was a good thing, as she would have no time to daydream over the Tirol. Her friends were astounded by the change in her and were so envious when her future plans were revealed. She soon got into her old habits of socialising with them and the Tirol seemed like a million miles away. With her mother's admittance into hospital only days away it suddenly dawned on Amelia how much she relied on her mum being there to comfort and give her wisdom and love unconditionally. Now it was Amelia's turn to show just how much she cared and how she was ready to take over the responsibility of running the hotel. She knew her father – this big strong macho man – would go to pieces while his wife was in hospital. He would be the last to admit it but he was nothing without his Eileen, but Amelia and her mother both knew this.

The summer seemed to drag along, even though it was very busy. Eileen's operation had been a complete success and she was going from strength to strength, to the relief of Amelia and her father. Jill had written regularly keeping her up with the village gossip. She remarked on Marcus's Swedish girlfriend who had been in Bachl the previous year but this time was staying at his house and had already been there for three weeks. Amelia couldn't help but feel a pang of envy. She did not like the way her mixed emotions played tricks on her, and tried to put these thoughts out of her head – but not very successfully! Had Jill been aware of the impact this information would have on her, she would never have included it in her letter but she had no idea Amelia still had feelings for Marcus.

On one of Amelia's nights out with her friends, Alex had joined the group and sheepishly asked how she was, even though it was obvious she was thriving, in fact he couldn't get over the change in her. He couldn't put his finger on it but in all the time he had known her he had never seen this side to her. She was so confident, amusing and contented. She had positively blossomed! He also realised he had blown it. He had always hoped they might get together as they were before, but now knew there was no chance of that ever happening. She was polite to him but kept him at arm's length, leaving him in no doubt that she had a new life, which did not include him!

When the season came to an end and the hotel had closed at the end of October, Amelia found she did not like having time on her hands and decided she would not wait until the end of November to return to Bachl. This would enable her to do some sightseeing. Her mother was now fully fit and was planning a coach trip with Charles to Edinburgh where they had friends. It was a regular thing and they tried to persuade Amelia to go with them, when she hit on the idea of returning earlier to the Tirol. Her mother could not help but notice the happiness in her face as she told them her changed plans, and wondered if there was something, or rather somebody, that had brought this change about her. Amelia had told her about village life and this Marcus seemed to crop up often in the conversation, but there was also a Luc whom she seemed very fond of but insisted they were both just friends. But this did not stop Eileen reading something into it. She knew her daughter well and usually she would be the first to know if there was a serious relationship, but even so...

12

Mid-November found Amelia all packed and more than ready to go, and apart from feeling sad at leaving her parents – especially her mother – she couldn't wait to leave cold, dark, windy old England behind. November and January must be the most depressing months in this country she thought, with the month of December being the happy month in between with the preparation and anticipation of Christmas, which she always loved. After once again saying her goodbyes she caught the train for Dover, where she boarded the ferry and once at Calais found the Arlberg Express waiting. She had not met any nice travelling companions like last time and felt extremely guilty over losing that lovely girl Eloise's address. What a pity she had not managed to give her hers as she would have loved to keep in touch and tell her how her holiday had materialised into a complete change of life.

Waking up and peering out of the window she saw the familiar mountains. They were now covered in snow, but only on the peaks. It was overcast but to Amelia's eyes it was a beautiful sight. 'I would love these views even if it were pouring with rain,' she said out loud. She had the compartment all to herself and by the time she had quickly dressed the coffee and croissants had arrived. She sat back and felt so happy she thought her heart would burst. As the train rolled into the station at Innsbruck she stuck her head out of the window and was surprised to see Luc standing there grinning. 'What a coincidence you happen to be at the station on the same platform as my train,' she said as he gave her a hug. 'Where are you off to?'

'Actually, I am here to pick you up,' he replied looking very pleased with himself.

'How on earth did you find out when I was arriving?' she asked, obviously taken aback.

'I was up in Bachl last week as it was such lovely weather so I popped into the tourist office and asked Franz, who by the way I have known for years, when you would be back. He not only told me the date but also the time of your arrival. So I suggested that as I live in Innsbruck I would pick you up to save him the journey. I hope you don't mind!'

'No, of course not, I'm sorry if I seemed a bit surprised, it was because I am, but nevertheless delighted'. After packing his car up with her luggage he opened the door and saw her safely seated. Amelia was still in a bit of a shock at seeing him and even more so when she saw his car – a huge white Mercedes – it all seemed a bit unreal. As was the norm, they chatted away nineteen to the dozen, quite comfortable in each other's company. Luc pulled in to the Wienerwald restaurant along the Autobahn and after refreshments hit the road for Bachl with Amelia now feeling light-headed from the mountain air, helped along with a glass of wine. Luc pulled up outside her flat, helped her inside with her luggage, shook hands with Maria and left, after telling Amelia he would be in touch. She had barely time to thank him before he was gone.

Maria enthusiastically showed her how everything worked in the flat and told her how happy she was to have her for the winter. If there was anything she wanted she need only ask. Amelia's eyes swept around the lovely flat with its wall to wall pine ceilings and floors, with matching cupboards and fitted wardrobes and fresh flowers on the table. There was a pretty, tiled bathroom and a small kitchen with a radio. From her balcony she had views across the valley to Innerbachl, which nestled amongst larch, spruce and pine trees. She knew she was going to be very happy here!

After a couple of days of settling in to her new flat and catching up with all her old friends, Amelia decided to go to Innsbruck to buy a typewriter in order to prepare the Guest Information books once the seminar was over. She decided against phoning Luc to tell him she was coming and instead had a day to herself during which she wandered around the old town and visited the Volkmuseum and the Hofburg palace and gardens and eventually the tourist office, where they were very friendly and informative. She was loaded up with her new portable typewriter (which was the current 1966 model and more expensive that she had intended), A4 paper and a wealth of brochures, which the tourist office had supplied her with. She caught the train back to Bergbrucke, from where she joined the Postbus for the last leg to Bachl. She had really enjoyed her day and couldn't wait to get back to her flat to browse over her little hoard and her notes. It was a godsend having a kitchen as it meant she did not have to go out for meals. In between seasons her food was her responsibility but in season she could have her meals at any of the hotels that the tour operator used. This was a perk of the job and one that was very necessary as there was no time to shop and prepare meals when the winter was in full swing. Her first-hand knowledge of the village, hotels and Gasthofs allocated to her was a boon and after the seminar she would have to visit each one to familiarise herself with the routine. She knew she would have to sort out excursions and transfers with Georg as well, and realised how fortunate she was to already have a working knowledge of the duties of a rep – thanks to Jill!

In the spare time she had before she attended the seminar at Seefeld, Amelia visited all the resorts she knew she would be taking excursions to during the winter: Salzburg, Krimml waterfalls, Rattenberg, Innsbruck and Sterzing/Vipitano. She collected brochures, postcards and lots of local history from each place and was well armed by the time she went to Seefeld. Her Saturday evenings were spent with the same old bowling crowd who roped her in for their jaunts to the bowling alley in the Ziller Valley. Marcus, while still being very friendly, was distinctly cooler. Amelia put this down to him having another interest, namely the Swedish girl that Jill had written about but who had long since gone. She still felt very drawn to him and wished she could understand her feelings, but one thing she did know was that she did not want a close relationship with him.

December finally arrived and with it the long-awaited seminar. Because British Airways appreciated their reps and looked after them if they did their jobs properly, she was the only new one there. The same reps would be in Tirol winter and summer until they wanted a change, to perhaps one of the resorts in the Tirol or even another country such as Italy, France or Switzerland. It was like one big family and even though it was intense and thorough, the seminar was an eye-opener. Amelia had no idea of the responsibility and what was expected of her but she knew she could most definitely handle it. She did not contact Luc as she literally did not have the time. The evenings were spent at the hotel where, after dinner, they would all gather in the bar and swap stories and information. They were a great crowd and by the time the seminar had finished Amelia was very much one of the team. Mike, who was the rep for Mayrhofen, insisted on giving her a lift back to Bachl as she had so much luggage by way of ski uniform, information book sleeves and lots of paperwork. The uniform consisted of red, white and blue anorak, white shirts, navy guernseys and black trousers. Very smart!

She was overjoyed once back in the village to hear from Maria that the other reps had arrived, and after quickly dropping off her bits and pieces she went to find Jill. She didn't have to look very far as she was in the Post with the other reps who were, she found, the same ones as had been there the previous winter. It was a happy reunion with, it seemed, everyone talking at once. They arranged to meet for an evening meal at the Alpenhof, with Jill saying she would come up to meet Amelia, as she wanted to see her flat. After their meal they discussed the rota for excursions and made notes about who was doing what and when, so they could now get on with the huge task of putting their information books together. Amelia had nine to do and was raring to go!

The first guests were due to arrive on the sixteenth of December. As yet there was only snow on the high peaks of the mountains but it had been promised for mid-week. Amelia worked hard at the info books, hours and hours of typing, cutting and placing. She found it was not a job that could be rushed and was just glad she had the time to do them justice. While in the middle of this mammoth task, with the nine books spread out on her bed and the table and chairs piled with the inserts she noticed it had become darker, looked out of the window and saw the reason – SNOW – great big fluffy flakes falling thick and fast! She went out on her balcony to watch this long-awaited, and welcome sight. 'Hallelujah!' she said out loud and went back to finish her task.

It had taken five full days but the finished products were well worth the extra effort she thought, feeling very pleased with herself. She decided against delivering them to the hotels while it was still snowing but instead delivered the rooming lists and put the noticeboard information up in the reception areas. She checked the rooming lists with the hotel owners and found them all so helpful and nice. She had been offered coffee and gateaux at every single place but after the first two politely declined. She found it was an insult to refuse refreshments but after explaining she had already eaten at the previous hotels was forgiven and offered Schnapps instead. By the time she headed back to her flat some four hours later after drinking three Schnapps and two glasses of wine to be polite, she was nearly away with the fairies!

It was still snowing the next day so in her anorak, ski trousers and moon boots and armed with her umbrella she took the first four books, as they were too heavy and bulky to manage more, and with her brolly up walked from hotel to hotel. She had to stop and shake the umbrella off regularly as it became heavy with snow, but felt a bit conspicuous, as no one else appeared to be using one. Marcus laughed when he saw her and said, 'You look so English *Millilein*, no one uses an umbrella out here unless it's raining. What do you think your anorak hood is for?'

She explained that she had to keep her books dry, to which he suggested that she wrap them in plastic bags and borrow a toboggan from Maria to transport them.

'Marcus! You are a genius,' she replied. 'I would never have thought of that!'

'Not a genius *Millilein*, just a Tirolean,' he said with a laugh.

13

The big day arrived and, dressed in her very smart uniform and shod in snow boots, Amelia met Georg at the transfer bus in the village centre. She had butterflies in her tummy and started to panic inwardly. Georg could see she was nervous and chatted away to her all the way to Munich airport. He gave her a lot of useful tips and assured her she would make a first class rep. The airport was two hours away but the journey passed more quickly than she expected as when Georg wasn't chatting she was going over and over her notes.

At the airport she met up with her colleagues from BA and awaited the throng due to appear from passport control. Amelia held up her clipboard with BACHL on it and very soon had her first crowd of guests. After picking their bags up from the carousel she led them to their coach. Once they were seated she did a head count and double-checked that everyone on her coach was for Bachl and not another resort. Satisfied, she instructed Georg to hit the road. She picked up the mike, stood up facing her guests, saw all the smiling faces looking at her and introduced herself and Georg, then welcomed them. She broke the ice by telling them sincerely that they were so lucky as they had chosen the most beautiful village not just in the Tirol but in all of Austria and she was there to make sure their holiday was all they hoped it would be. She started off by telling them a little of the village in general and the local customs, of the friendliness, cleanliness and interesting and varied menus awaiting them in their hotels. She continued with the location of the doctor's surgery, telephones and ski school, meal times, trips out and evening entertainment. When the coach stopped at the border checkpoint with the Tirol she went around the bus giving out maps and leaflets of village information, plus booking forms for the day and evening activities. Once cleared of the border she welcomed them to the Tirol, said she appreciated they must be tired so they could now nod off if they wanted, and put a new James Last tape on. She sat back in her seat with a sigh of relief, and Georg, who had been listening to but not understanding everything she had talked about, told her that if he did not know differently he would have sworn she had been doing it for years! This really boosted her confidence and she just hoped the rest of the transfer went as smoothly.

Once in the village the coach dropped the guests off at their various hotels, all armed with timetables of when they were due at the ski-hire shop. She stressed how important it was to keep to their timetable otherwise the shop would become overcrowded, and also that they would not have to wait too long this way. Afterwards, she would be at the Post hotel where a large table was allocated to her in a corner of the dining room and this was where she would be every day from 6 to 7.30 pm. These were her 'office hours' for any queries, problems or bookings for day and evening entertainment. They could also contact her in an emergency through the tourist office, who could find out where she was. There were more guests arriving on a later flight from Manchester and they were brought to the village by Georg and his daughter Elsa who did the on-board commentary. It all went on wheels but the 'office hours' went on until 9 pm, partly due to booking the day and evening activities but mostly because of excited guests who were overwhelmed by it all, especially the picture-postcard village, and wanted to keep on asking questions which she was only too pleased to answer.

Jill had popped her head around the door several times and catching Amelia's eye pointed at the time. Amelia nodded and very politely excused herself by reminding her guests she had not eaten since lunchtime, but would see them all at the information meeting at 11 am the next day. Jill reproached her for allowing it to drag on and advised her to take this first transfer as a lesson, to put her foot down and really stress to her guests on the transfer coach that the 'office hours' on Saturdays were strictly for bookings. They could ask any questions they wanted at the Sunday morning information meeting, where each person could hear the questions and answers as a crowd. Amelia listened intently and realised Jill was giving her very good advice. She was absolutely starving, but before she could do anything else she had to ring Georg with the numbers for the days and evening events. Georg complimented her on her superb transfer but also told her that the numbers should be in by 8 and not 9.15 pm! Amelia apologised and explained what had happened and that Jill had already put her on the right path. During their late supper, Amelia gave Jill a full account of her day and they arranged to meet each other after the sleigh ride that Amelia was taking the next afternoon.

The information meeting went really well and she was relieved to find all her guests were happy with their hotels and meals. Afterwards she visited all nine hotels and Gasthofs to check everything was in order. It was nearly 3 pm and time for the sleigh ride by the time she had completed her 'rounds', so Amelia made straight for the meeting point in the village centre. Josef, who managed the sleigh rides, had the maximum twelve sleighs lined up with the horses ready to go. Each sleigh held four

90

people, which meant that if guests had not booked there would be no chance of them joining on the spur of the moment. The rugs were placed over their knees and after a head count Amelia joined the last one for this, her first sleigh ride.

The horses followed the road a little way through the village then cut across the fields where they could go at a faster pace. Suddenly there was loud and prolonged farting coming from the horses which, being British and reserved, the guests at first pretended not to hear. There were just muffled giggles and snorts until one lady couldn't hold back any longer and just screamed out laughing at which everyone with great relief joined in. Amelia had noticed the men holding the reins and controlling the brakes on the sleighs slyly grinning at one another. The people that had been eager to get the front seats were now rather regretting it due to the excessive amount of wind!

They eventually joined the road for the steep, winding climb up to the Alpenruhe with the sleighs' runners neatly fitting into the icy ruts of the road. As they climbed higher and higher the temperature dropped lower and lower. The horses ploughed along through the dense trees and after half an hour, as the sun began to set, horses and guests arrived at the Alpenruhe.

After their passengers had alighted, the horses were led into the barn where they were fed and watered in readiness for the return journey. Following Amelia into the Alpenruhe the guests were met by the wonderful aroma of Gluhwein – hot mulled red wine spiced with cinnamon, cloves and slivers of lemon and orange peel and sugar. The spectacular views of the village, which by now was a group of twinkling lights far in the valley below, were enhanced by the distant shadows of the northernmost chain of the Alps as a backdrop. Above them the sky was pitch black, unspoilt by the yellowy haze common in more built-up areas. Thousands upon thousands of stars and a clear view of the Milky Way added to the magic, and this was crowned with the Gluhwein and entertainment in the form of dancing, harp, concertina, guitar and yodelling – it was heady stuff! Everybody, including Amelia, was in high spirits and when the time came, no one wanted to leave.

They left the Alpenruhe after much hand-shaking and thanking of the family, out to their waiting sleighs. Josef had earlier explained the procedure for the return. Using her torch, Amelia was to start off at Josef's sleigh which was the lead, and check each one to make sure everyone was there. When she came to the last one she was to shout 'Complete Josef!' and away they would go. Following his instructions she checked every sleigh and seeing by the time she was almost at hers that everyone was accounted for she shouted 'Complete Josef!' In a flash the sleighs pulled off one after another, going at speed downhill. It was by now pitch dark with no moon and only the little lanterns on the sleighs to light their way.

Suddenly Amelia realised she should have been on the last one and it was quickly disappearing down the hill with absolutely no chance of her catching it up! No one could hear her shouts as the swishing of the sleighs cutting through the ice and snow, together with the loud singing of Jingle Bells, completely drowned her out. She stood mortified, watching the twinkling lights and hearing the happy singing disappearing down the winding road. She was too embarrassed to go back into the Alpenruhe, so started picking her way gingerly along the ruts in the road, falling over again and again. She was so cold, her feet felt like lumps of ice despite her moon boots. The faint outline of the branches on the trees overhead gave her the creeps, her imagination ran haywire! She battled on and eventually arrived at her flat, which, thank God, was on the Alpenruhe side of the village. It had taken her two hours whereas, on the sleigh, coming down was normally ten minutes or so. She burst into tears as soon as she was inside the door, pulled herself together, had a quick shower to warm herself up, borrowed Maria's toboggan and was in the village in record time!

At the Post, the guests who had been waiting to see her at her 'office hours' had been wondering where she was and had returned several times hoping to catch her. When eventually she arrived she was already armed with the excuse that she had been called away to an emergency which she was not at liberty to divulge! This was accepted, with the guests dying to know what the emergency had been. She would rather die than anyone should find out the truth, with the exception of Jill who tried to keep a straight face but in the end just had to scream out laughing when Amelia explained the sorry story to her. In between this uncontrollable laughter, and with tears in her eyes which spilled onto her cheeks, Jill tried to apologise and instead of Amelia feeling upset, Jill's laughter was so contagious she joined in. With their emotions now under control, Amelia told her about the farting horses, and Jill enlightened her by explaining that wily Josef always fed the horses a good helping of beans before a sleigh ride, as he and his men loved watching the reaction of the Brits. He reckoned it made the journey more interesting – but he did not do it for the Germans! As it was a regular thing Jill advised her never to sit immediately behind the horse but as far back in the line up as possible. Amelia made a mental note of this!

The next morning she met her guests at the ski-school meeting place and had already armed them with what to expect – how they would be allocated instructors and then have two hours' tuition, a two hour lunch break before regrouping, then a further two hours. She had advised them that if they needed the shops or supermarkets during the lunch break to forget it, as the shops all shut at twelve noon until 2 pm. Any shopping must be done before ski school as the shops were all open at 7.30 am. Après ski was at every hotel and a good way of unwinding and socialising. She also warned them of the vicious kick of Jagertee and to avoid the temptation, as it would floor them. She explained that even though it tasted delicious it had nothing whatsoever to do with tea; it was in fact mulled red wine with Schnapps, rum and sugar. On the other hand, Gluhwein was a wonderful drink when you come in from the cold, as the guests who had been on the sleigh ride had found out. She handed out the lift passes, wished them luck and advised them not to drink too much at lunch time as there were no loos on the slopes.

She breakfasted with the other reps and once the last-minute details of the excursions had been organised they all went off to do their mounds of paperwork. It involved phoning the coach contractor with final numbers for excursions, then ringing the hotels and venues to book the fondue, raclette, bowling, slide-show, farmhouse and Tirolean evenings. By the time she had finished it was too late to go skiing so she went to visit Gretl and Georg instead. The Konditorei was quiet due to nearly everyone being on the slopes, which gave her a chance to have a chat with Gretl. She learned there had been a big row between Marcus and his family, as he had insisted on being a ski instructor instead of getting on with his tailoring business and his many orders. Apparently it was Marcus's sister Erna who had relayed this information to Gretl, who told Amelia how glad she was that she was not mixed up with him. Erna had also said that Marcus was drinking too much again and the family had been dead against the Swedish girl staying there in summer but Marcus had reminded them that not only was he the only son but it was his inheritance they were living in. This had caused ructions with his parents, but was absolutely true.

'Mark my words Milli, when his parents are no longer here he will lose his business as its only his father that keeps it going in the winters.'

On hearing this Amelia felt quite depressed and said how sorry she was to hear that such a clever man could be so foolish. Finishing her coffee with a promise that she would see them again soon, she made for the Krone bar, knowing full well Marcus would be there after ski school along with most of the other instructors.

'Hello *Millilein*, had a good day?'

'Yes thanks, busy but good, how about you?' she asked concerned.

'Fine, fine, I was glad to see you coping so well with your guests this morning, I have several of them in my group and they all speak very highly of you.'

'That's nice to hear Marcus. I have a lovely crowd and only hope it continues like this throughout the winter then I will be a very happy bunny.'

He smiled wistfully at her and said, 'What does a man have to do to get that sort of attention from you, because if I knew how I would be right at the front of the queue!'

This really caught her off guard. As she did not know how to reply she gave him a smile and patted his shoulder as she got up to leave, with the excuse she had her 'office hours' to get to.

14

Christmas Eve. Amelia's first week's guests had departed and new guests had arrived the day before with another successful transfer. With the people who had stayed on from the first week she had a full compliment. Added to her usual information meeting she had told her guests that the twenty-fourth of December was the day that the Continentals celebrated Christmas, and the shops would be shut at 5 pm to enable the families to celebrate. They would have a sumptuous meal followed by carols around the tree and the opening of presents. The sleigh ride was booked once again to capacity. Once everyone was seated Amelia jumped on the last sleigh, only to be joined by Marcus who appeared out of the blue and squeezed himself next to her. Josef had seen this and gave him a nod and they were off. Before Amelia could say anything, Marcus explained that he had to deliver and collect Christmas presents for his family from the Alpenruhe and he hoped she didn't mind. The truth was she did not mind one little bit.

The guests were all in high spirits, it was all so magical – pristine snow, clear sky, millions of stars, the jingling of the bells around the horses' necks and the moment she had been bracing herself for once they started to cross the field – the farting! As before, there was an embarrassed silence before a thunderous belly laugh from one of the male guests. In a matter of seconds there was contagious laughter followed by the singing of Jingle Bells as they approached the ascent to the Alpenruhe. It was a real Christmassy evening and something the guests would never forget. Marcus too was in high spirits and was welcomed enthusiastically by the family who, like all villagers, were lifelong friends.

They all had a great time and were once again reluctant to leave, but not before Amelia reminded them about the church service at 11 pm and the brass band that would be playing on the Post balcony immediately afterwards. This time on the return journey she made sure she was seated before shouting 'Complete Josef!' The horses hurtled down the mountain, glad to stretch their legs after the slow ascent, and Amelia was aware of the closeness of Marcus who made sure the blanket was over both their knees.

'You really are making such a wonderful job of this, *Millilein*, it's like this is what you were born to do,' he shouted above the singing.

'That's right Marcus, that's absolutely how I feel about it too,' she shouted back.

The sleighs came to a halt in the village centre but before she could say anything Marcus had hopped off, given her a peck on the cheek, said, 'See you in the Post after the brass band' and was gone. She met the other reps for the church service and afterwards they watched the candle-lit procession and joined what seemed like the whole village in the square in front of the Post. The brass band appeared and, even though the reps knew what to expect, once they started playing 'Silent Night' the throng went quiet and the tears began to flow, it was all so beautiful and surreal. Marcus was playing the tuba, which didn't fail to impress her. Was there no end to this man's talents?

The reps jostled their way up to the bar and ordered large Gluhweins. The British army joined them. Amelia had not had any time to socialise with them since arriving back from the seminar. She was glad to see Mike Jones again but found it impossible to have a conversation because it was so noisy. She promised she would meet up with him once the festivities were over. Marcus was with a whole crowd of people, which she was glad about as she did not want to be singled out. The reps were probably the first to leave as they reminded each other that it was 'business as usual tomorrow'!

15

Christmas Day. A normal ski school day, which meant that after doing the rounds of her hotels Amelia had time to herself to ski. She happily arrived at the blue run feeling confident that by now she could cope with the bumps. Just as she was about to descend she heard her name called out by a familiar voice. 'Come and join my team *Millilein*.' It could be no other than Marcus, who always seemed to suddenly appear out of the woodwork when she least expected it! So as not to embarrass him by refusing, she reluctantly skied over to his group, smiled and said hello to them all, and inwardly said a silent prayer that she would not make a fool of herself again. Her prayers were answered as she effortlessly kept up with the group, navigating the bumps and narrow tracks with ease. When she reached the bottom with a swish of her skis and a perfect parallel stop she took off her goggles to the amused and astonished look of the handsome man with laughing green eyes. 'Well done *Millilein*, that was superb, are you coming up again?' he asked, to which she replied that she had to get back as she was having a late lunch with the reps, which was perfectly true. She went back to her flat, put her glad rags on, redid her make-up and at four o'clock as arranged met up with the girls for their special lunch at the Alpenhof.

They were all in high spirits, the flashes of homesickness long gone as they tucked into the enormous feast. They all agreed that they must be amongst the luckiest girls in the world to be in such a wonderful place and doing a job which they loved. Lunch over, they went into the huge bar where, at the far end, was a larger than average log fire spitting and crackling as it roared up the chimney. Halfway up the room stood an enormous Christmas tree festooned with red ribbons, silver bells and lots of twinkling golden lights. At six o'clock on the dot there was a call for silence as a group who had positioned themselves in the corner started to sing Silent Night and the lights slowly dimmed. As soon as they finished singing and before people realised what was happening there was the sound of sleigh bells. The French doors suddenly opened and there outside was Father Christmas on his horse-drawn sleigh, with lots of sacks of presents. All the children that were staying at the Alpenhof together with many others were dumbstruck, their little faces a picture of wonderment as Father Christmas took his place by the tree and the sacks were placed next to him. To the accompanying voices of the little choir singing a range of English Christmas carols he called out children's names and one by one they shyly walked up, absolutely and totally mesmerised as he wished them a Happy Christmas, then handed them a present with their name on. This continued until all the presents were given out and to the chorus of Jingle Bells he jumped on his sleigh, smiling and waving as it swished away. How all this came about was the brainchild of the hotel owner who had informed the guests with children that Father Christmas would be arriving and if they wanted him to give a present to their child then they must wrap one up, put the child's name on it and hand it in to reception. She stipulated it must remain all hush-hush to add to the magic of it all. The parents readily agreed and did as they were told, but even they had a huge surprise the way it was so beautifully organised. There were many happy tears amongst the grown-ups who were watching as their children went forward as if in a daze when their name was called out. Most were speechless. The happy tears were from the adults, including the reps, but *not* the children!

During their 'office hours' the reps had reminded their guests of the English Carol service that was taking place in the Church at 11 pm and had been organised by the British Army Ski Association. The church and the huge Christmas tree in front of it were illuminated, and loud-speakers positioned outside to enable everyone who was not fortunate enough to get a seat inside to follow the service. It was very cold on the feet standing there, however this was quickly rectified by the visitors, locals and reps alike nipping into the Post to replenish their jugs of Gluhwein. This was the procedure every year and the service was eagerly attended not only by the Brits of every denomination but the locals who joined in the singing whether they knew the words or not, the main thing was they knew the melodies and loved them!

Once again just before midnight, when everyone had poured out onto the square, the lights on the upper balcony of the Post came on and the band appeared, to ecstatic applause. The villagers passed candles among the crowd and the teenage girls of the band dispensed Schnapps from little barrels on a belt around their waists. At midnight on the dot the band started to play Silent Night. It all felt very magical and emotionally charged. You could hear a pin drop from the crowd where there was not a dry eye amongst them. To deafening applause the band played their encore of 'O Tannenbaum' to which everyone joined in. The band then had to stop due to their lips sticking to their instruments in the icy cold. Afterwards most of the locals went home but the holidaymakers poured into the hotel bars. The reps decided to turn in as they had their work to do the next day. They all agreed this was the only way and in the only place they ever wanted to spend Christmas!

16

Another week was whizzing by with happy and satisfied guests and soon it was Saturday again and airport transfer day. This too went smoothly until the head count on the coach, when Amelia found there was one missing guest among the new arrivals. She quickly scanned her list for single bookings of which there were three in total. She asked the single booking guests to put their hand up when she called their names and quickly saw that the missing person was a Paul Mitchell. She apologised for the delay and explained that she would have to go back into the arrivals hall as she had obviously missed him somehow. Fortunately Anne-Marie was still there and went on the tannoy system calling his name and asking that he would go as quickly as possible to the information desk, but to no avail. If he had got on the wrong bus he would have been sent to the right one before it departed, but as they both saw, there was only one bus that had not left and that was the Bachl one. They waited for another five minutes and when he didn't turn up Anne-Marie said there had been no last-minute cancellations and gave Amelia the go-ahead to leave, after pointing out that if by any chance he was still at the airport then he would have to get a taxi at his own expense.

All this hullabaloo had held the coach up for more than half an hour and when Amelia returned to the coach she found Klaus the driver standing waiting for her. 'That missing idiot arrived here drunk ten minutes after you left and is on the coach fast asleep,' he said angrily. When she saw Paul Mitchell slumped in his seat with his head against the window dead to the world and a dribble running down his chin she decided to leave him as there was nothing whatever she could do at that precise moment – *but wait until they were in the village* and then he would get a piece of her mind! She once again apologised to her guests and told them to try and ignore him, unless of course he started to snore then that would be a different matter! She did her commentary and everything went fine until they arrived very late in the village. The delay had knocked out the routine for the ski hire and they had gone on to fitting other guests. At her belated 'office hours' there were a few disgruntled people but she promised them it would only get better and this was not a normal occurrence. It was after ten o'clock when she finally had the last guests sorted out, except for that wretched Paul who had not even been for his ski hire. The last she had seen of him was when she woke him up with a good shake of his shoulder and he snorted and opened two red eyes, not knowing where the hell he was. He had been told in no uncertain terms to go to his hotel room and freshen up. She gave him the information list that would tell him anything he needed to know regarding his holiday, so it was up to him to get himself sorted out once he had read it. She was not going to chase after him as her responsibility was towards the other guests.

There was no sign of him for the next few days so Amelia asked the guests who were staying at his hotel if they had seen him, and the reply was he was at the evening meals looking unkempt and keeping very much to himself. As he had not attended the ski school which he had booked she left a message at his hotel for him to come and see her between 6 and 7.30 at her 'office hours' but he never bothered. After a discussion with Anne-

Marie she was told she could do no more but to make sure he understood if he was not at reception at the stated time of departure, the transfer bus would leave without him, which would mean he would have to pay for a taxi to the airport out of his own pocket and just hope he could be accommodated on another flight! With this information under her belt Amelia left another note for the wretched man, this time pushing it under his door. The week was going very well again until Thursday morning when, on the way to the tourist office she was confronted by a scruffy, unshaven, red-eyed Paul – stinking of stale booze. She asked where he had been for the last five days and why had he not acknowledged her messages. He replied that he had been enjoying himself with some friends but wanted a refund for his ski hire and ski school as he had not used them.

'I'm afraid you will have to take that up with BA when you get back as you booked and pre-paid for them in the UK,' she replied.

'But I have to have that money now, especially as I have lost my wallet,' he said angrily.

'Have you reported it to the police Paul, as that is the first thing you should do?'

'No, not yet but I have to have money right now so you will have to lend it to me.'

She firmly told him there was no way she was allowed to lend him money but that she would get straight on to her boss and ask what the procedure was. In the meantime she told him to go up to the police station and report the loss and she would meet him in an hour in the Jagerhof.

'I will wait until you have spoken with your boss but make sure she understands my dilemma as I must have some money one way or another. I will wait for you here,' he said as he folded his arms and sat on the wall by the church.

She explained to Franz what had happened and was allowed to use the phone there to get straight on to Anne-Marie, who was not in the least surprised when she heard the full story. 'That's an old con trick Amelia, I have come across it several times. As for his refund, tell him I shall send a report to our HQ in the UK and they will deal with it. He obviously hasn't read the small print as it clearly states it is non-refundable, but for goodness sake don't tell him that, we'll leave it to Head Office! Regarding his missing wallet, take him to the police station but point out beforehand to make sure his wallet really is missing as the police do not take too kindly to people wasting their time. He must then go to the bank and get them to contact his bank in the UK and arrange for money to be transferred to him straight away, but please emphasise it takes time so the sooner he goes the quicker he will get some money through, and please make it quite clear there is absolutely no possibility of him having a borrow off you!'

When Amelia met Paul and passed on what her boss had said, he just shrugged his shoulders, said he would make another search of his room and started to walk away. 'Please let me know how you get on, Paul, you know where and at what time my office hours are,' she called after him but he never even turned around and just kept walking.

She did not see him again until the transfer on Saturday morning where much to her surprise he was with the other guests all ready to go. 'How did you get on at the police station Paul, and did you manage to get your money through from the bank?' she asked, concerned. Still unkempt and stinking of stale booze he replied that he had found his wallet but he had an even greater problem. He took her to one side and said he had a problem 'down below'.

106

'What the hell are you talking about?' she asked suspiciously, to which he replied, 'Well my willy is sore and terribly swollen – look!'

At which point he started to unzip his trousers.

'DON'T YOU DARE!!' she almost shouted. 'Now pull yourself together, get on the coach and behave yourself. There is a medical centre at the airport which I shall take you to.'

The other guests were dying to know what was going on but Amelia, in a very professional tone, assured them it was nothing, and they really must get a move on as they were already behind schedule.

17

After what seemed like months, but in fact had only been three weeks, Leni, the Swedish woman who had been staying with Marcus, appeared no more. It seemed to Amelia that she was always popping up in the same places that *she* frequented, and always with her arm around Marcus like a prize trophy. It didn't help that not only did she have the most fashionable clothes and a svelte figure, she was also drop-dead gorgeous. Together they were a very handsome pair! It made Amelia feel frumpy and inadequate, and unnerved her to realise she had these unwanted emotions and really did not know how to cope with them. She knew she could not even think of a serious relationship with him as they were two completely different people and it would never come to anything, not only because of their different religions – Catholic and Church of England – but also their different cultures. She could not, and would not, ever succumb to being a stay-at-home wife while her husband was socialising, as was the custom. She was emancipated and did not envy the wives and girlfriends, especially in the ski season! She tried to apply this logic to her better nature but had to admit there was some great attraction to Marcus that she couldn't shake off, not for want of trying! It was too late now anyway as it was obvious to her that Marcus was heavily involved with the Swede.

Anne-Marie arrived with her new contract for the summer season and told Amelia how pleased she was with her progress. Now that she was well and truly established there would be an increase in her wages. She also told Amelia the procedure for the last winter departures and gave her the choice of travelling back to the UK with these departures or, if she wanted a few days to unwind and get her flat sorted out for the summer, she could have a flight the following week which would be the fourth of April. Amelia did not have to give her answer straight away if she wanted time to think about it, as long as she let her know by mid-week. Amelia indeed liked the idea of some quality time in the village with no guests to look after and plumped for the flight on the fourth. When Jill heard what she was doing she decided to do the same thing and came up with the suggestion that they take a short break to Rome, as there was a four-day trip by coach from Innsbruck on the twenty-eighth of March which she had only recently seen advertised in the local paper, the *Tiroler Tageszeitung*. Amelia jumped at the chance and left it to Jill to do the booking if there were still seats available. Jill went off and phoned and was back in a matter of minutes. It was all booked!

It was her turn to take the Innsbruck/Vipiteno excursion on Friday, a trip she always thoroughly enjoyed which took them to Vipiteno in the morning and Innsbruck for the afternoon. She told her passengers a little of the history of where they were going, and that Vipiteno was always signposted Sterzing/Vipiteno as it has once been part of Sud (south) Tirol, but was lost forever to Italy in 1919 when Italy won their war against the Austro-Hungarian Empire. Overnight, part of Sudtirol became part of northern Italy, which caused deep divisions for both those who had been annexed and those who remained in the Tirol. The main language was German, however only Italian was taught in the schools, thus all towns and villages in the former Sudtirol have signposts in both Italian and German.

It was a pretty drive to Vipiteno, and once they had passed Innsbruck they crossed the famous 620-foot high Europabrucke, then travelled along the motorway and many smaller bridges before crossing the border at the Brenner Pass into northern Italy. The scenery along the way was always appreciated by the passengers, especially with Amelia's informative running commentary.

After the Brenner Pass there was a series of fields sloping down the narrow valley, which were, a serious Amelia pointed out, the Pasta Fields – they had had a bumper harvest the previous autumn. There was a short silence, followed by a burst of laughter when they realised they had been conned. She continued her commentary with a brief history of the town of Sterzing/Vipiteno and pointed out that the high mountains surrounding the town have many deep caves, visible roughly half-way up. These, she explained, were no ordinary caves, but were in fact Treacle Mines, which were a boon to the Italian economy. Another silence, while most of the guests took stock of what she had just said, and weren't sure whether to believe it or not as she sounded so convincing. It didn't take them long to realise that they had been conned again, but once Amelia started talking about the thick exposed pipe in the field to their right, explaining it was the main wine pipe from Italy to the Tirol – red in the morning, white in the afternoons and rosé in the evenings – there was instantaneous laughter. She had the whole coach in the palm of her hand and they were like one big happy family.

At Sterzing/Vipiteno – the picturesque little town that had preserved its medieval character – there was a two-hour stay to enable her guests to buy their duty-free leather goods, cigarettes and alcohol, with time to sample the local pizza and pasta parlours before joining the coach again for the hour-long drive back to Innsbruck.

On arrival in Innsbruck, where they had a three-hour stay, Amelia issued each of her guests with a map of the town, with an 'x' marking the spot of the most important and interesting places, pointing out to allow plenty of time if they decided to visit the Olympic ski jump on the Bergisl mountain, as it was a tram ride away and then a good climb up to the top. Wishing them a pleasant afternoon, she pointed them in the direction of the Old Town and emphasised they must be back at the pick-up point on time as the traffic police were very strict and would move them on after the maximum ten minutes allotted for dropping off and picking up.

Whilst in Innsbruck she decided to go to the bank and get her Italian lire in preparation for Rome. After the transaction she was on her way out when coming up the steps towards her she saw Luc. He was as surprised as she was and when told she still had two hours in Innsbruck he asked her to wait a few minutes while he sorted out his business and then if she wanted they could go for a coffee or something stronger. He took her to the Hopfgarten – the palace gardens where there was a lovely rustic restaurant. He ordered two glasses of Sect, an Austrian champagne, and they sat chatting away until Amelia noticed the time and said she had to get back to the coach, but not before promising to phone him from Seefeld when she was back in the middle of May for the seminar. He told her he would take her to a famous fish restaurant with breathtaking views and where the trout were caught from their own lake. She sat on the coach on the return journey and tried to work out why this cultured darling man did not have the same attraction for her as Casanova Marcus. He was obviously well heeled, didn't drink to excess, didn't smoke, had a great sense of humour, treated her like a lady and was very, very attractive. He was like a breath of fresh air, added to the fact there were no strings! No matter how hard she tried to work it out she could not find the answer.

The Rome trip was a godsend as it gave Amelia something else to focus on. She was really excited at the prospect, especially as she was going with Jill. Until now, she had been enjoying the ski season, but she now started to look forward to its end. As March progressed, the snow was leaving the sunny side of the valley where the village was situated, but on the shaded side the chairlift ski area would have plenty of snow for several weeks to come. In the village, where only a few short weeks ago there had been snow-covered nursery slopes, there were now blankets of crocuses that seemed to have popped up overnight. The visitors were slowly thinning out, which left the reps with more time to themselves to indulge in skiing and sunning themselves at the top station. They all had bronzed faces with hair highlighted from the sun and were the picture of health. Amelia had avoided Marcus without making it obvious, but on the occasions they did meet he always treated her as if she was very special. She longed to ask him about Leni but was afraid of the answer and besides he might take it the wrong way and think she was jealous – as if!

One afternoon, as Amelia sat on her balcony, Jill arrived to give her the disturbing but not unexpected news that the body of Fritz had been found. He was lying face-down by the side of a fence on a steep field opposite the Liftstuberl. In his tipsy state he had obviously decided to take a short cut back to the village, and must have fallen whilst climbing over the fence. As it was in the bottom of the valley, the lack of sun for most of the day meant January's ice and snow would have made for very slippery conditions, added to the fact it had snowed for two days after he disappeared. He must have hit his head on a large stone which was found next to the body. If that wasn't bad enough, when the rescue team went to lift him up – still partly frozen – his face was left in the ice.

'His poor, poor mother,' said a shocked Amelia, to which Jill nodded.

Even though it was expected at some stage that his body would be found in the thaw it was very, very sad news and the girls noticed the sombre atmosphere when they walked into the Jagerhof at après ski time. Opposite, at the Chapel of Rest which adjoined the church, was a long queue of villagers who had come to pay their last respects. There was a large photo, as was the custom, and several wreaths lying on top of the closed coffin. It would be a three-day ritual before burial.

This was the third funeral Amelia had seen, and she remembered very well the first, which had been the previous year. It seemed like the whole village turned out, including the farming families that lived high up on the mountains. On the day of interment the coffin would be carried around the centre of the village preceded by the brass band playing soulful dirges. Behind the coffin came the immediate family followed by whichever Service the deceased belonged to, be it mountain rescue, ski instructor, fire brigade or brass band, all wearing the appropriate uniforms. Lastly came the villagers in droves. It was a spectacle that would not fail to touch even the hardest heart. After the service and interment in the graveyard the women went home while their menfolk headed into the Gasthof for the wake.

Koni the rascal, approached Amelia and Jill while they were sitting on the balcony of the Alpenhof one afternoon and invited them to a rabbit goulash at a farmhouse up the valley the following evening – but stipulated it was hush-hush as it was only for a select group which included themselves and some of the villagers. At first they were a bit suspicious, but he managed to convince them it was all above board and too good to miss! They accepted, after agreeing it was a bit of an honour and also a new experience for them both. They turned up at the farmhouse and were met by a delicious smell of cooking and the rest of the invited party. There was Marcus, Sepp, Fuzzi, Franz, Oswald and Traudl and her husband who owned the farmhouse. Franz and Koni were doing the cooking while Oswald strummed the guitar and Traudl played the squeezebox. The beer and wine were flowing and the girls found no difficulty in joining in the celebratory spirit. Marcus made no secret of his delight at the presence of the girls and made sure their glasses were always topped up!

By the time the meal was ready they were all three sheets to the wind and starving. The goulash was absolutely delicious and plentiful. After the meal they had a singsong but Marcus did not overstep the mark, which came as a bit of a surprise both to Jill and Amelia. After a really superb evening that the girls had wallowed in, it was time for the trek back to the village. When the girls left, the party was still ongoing. They thanked their hosts for the privilege of their invitation to the rabbit goulash and headed back to their flats. Jill remarked how she was surprised that Marcus had made no attempt to single Amelia out and reckoned it was because she was with her, but it didn't stop her noticing the loving way he looked at Amelia! They both agreed it had been an evening with a difference and giggled their way along the mountain path.

The following day Amelia was at her 'office hours', when Jill arrived and appeared out of breath. 'Mel, I must talk to you in private for a few minutes,' she whispered.

Amelia, noticing the urgency in Jill's voice, excused herself from her guests and followed her to a quiet corner. 'Mel, I have just heard that the police are looking for the thief who stole the two pet rabbits from the farm by the fire station!'

'Oh my God,' said an equally shocked Amelia.

Jill continued, 'There were footsteps in the snow leading across the garden and up to the hutch and then back out! It's too much of a coincidence that we were at a rabbit goulash party the same day as they had been taken so don't for God's sake mention to anyone where you were last night!' They were two shocked and worried Reps and agreed to keep mum.

When Amelia saw Marcus at the bar later just as she had sorted out her last guests she went up and whispered that she wanted to talk to him. He nodded and moved to a quiet area away from the bar. 'I've heard about the missing pet rabbits Marcus and I want the truth. Did you know where they had come from?'

'Not until I was actually at the farmhouse when I saw Koni laugh as he was preparing them for the pot. When Traudl suspiciously asked where he had got them from he said it was a big secret and the party must also be kept secret. That was just before you arrived.'

Amelia could not hide her disbelief and disgust at the thought that she had eaten and enjoyed someone's pet rabbit and told him so.

'You can believe me *Millilein* that had I known what he was up to I would have stopped him. If the police find out about the party we are all in trouble so it is vital you say nothing about it like the rest of us. As for Koni – it is typical! I just hope the police don't question him, as he is going to deny it. As there were no witnesses when he bagged them he knows damn well it would be more than our lives are worth if any of this gets out.'

115

'It was such a super evening Marcus, Jill and I were thrilled to be a part of village life with the locals instead of nearly always with our guests. You can believe me, when I see Koni I shall leave him in no doubt as to what Jill and I feel about thieving, pet murderers! I feel like a bloody cannibal knowing that I have eaten someone's beloved pets and Jill feels the same. We do not want to be involved and wild horses would not drag the truth out of us.'

There was no mistaking her anger and loathing, and because he thought she didn't believe his version of events he promised her on his mother's life that what he told her was the truth. On hearing this she instinctively reached out and touched his shoulder.

'I believe you, Marcus, but it is an explosive situation and if as reps we were involved in any police inquiries our jobs would be on the line so it is imperative we are kept out of it, please understand this.'

'*Millilein*, we are all sworn to secrecy so there is no chance the finger will be pointed at us. Now please come and have a drink with me to show there are no hard feelings.'

Jill arrived as they were sitting at the bar and Amelia told her they would talk about it later when there would be no chance of anyone overhearing. After accepting a drink from Marcus the three sat uncomfortably but discreetly looking around to see if there was any sign of their companions of the night before. It was unusual not to see Franz or Koni in the bar; they were obviously keeping their heads down. Walking home they both agreed it would now be a relief to be on that coach to Rome and it couldn't come quick enough!

After a few days the saga of the missing rabbits had gone very quiet, and although the police and a few others had their suspicions about Koni, nothing could be proved, especially as he had sworn it was nothing to do with him! There was no one more relieved than Amelia and Jill but they still felt uncomfortable with the situation. They took their minds off it by poring over brochures of what to do and see in a short time in Rome.

At last the day of the final departing guests arrived. After waving her last guests off at Munich airport, Amelia took the opportunity of the empty coach and two-hour drive to catch up on her paperwork. They were leaving for Rome the following morning, and the paperwork had to be sent off immediately to Anne-Marie.

18

Jill had been to Rome twice before but was still as excited as her first time. On the day they joined their coach at Innsbruck they were on top of the world and full of anticipation over the coming days. They were amused to find that out of an almost-full coach they were the only Brits, the rest appearing to be either German or Austrian, and consisting mostly of females. The back seat was taken up by five of these ladies, who introduced themselves to Jill and Amelia and told them they owned Gasthofs in a village outside Innsbruck and this was their annual pilgrimage as soon as the ski season was over. Their ears pricked up when they found that the girls were both reps as they knew how important their work was to the hotel industry – a good rep meant satisfied guests. It was a twelve-hour journey, with frequent stops for refreshments. The huge, spotlessly clean and tastefully decorated restaurants along the motorway were a far cry from the ones in the UK. The assortment of food was mind-boggling. For lunch they plumped for the carvery, where there was a suckling pig on a spit and a choice of hot and cold meats, and a huge assortment of vegetables, salad, rice and pasta. With their plates piled high they tucked in hungrily, giving each other satisfied smiles as they ploughed through the mouth-watering food. They were well and truly unwinding!

Amelia was awe-struck at her first sight of Rome as they came over the brow of a hill. It was early evening and the buildings were bathed in the red glow of the setting sun. Jill pointed out the seven hills, and seeing her friend's delight and enthusiasm, knew she was going to enjoy showing her the sights.

The hotel was centrally located, and the huge foyer had beautiful marble floors. In fact, the floors throughout the hotel were all marble. Jill explained that the buildings were created to withstand the heat and the marble floors were a way of combatting it. They walked for miles and had their bottoms pinched more than once. At the Vatican City Amelia was bowled over by the paintings and sculptures of Michelangelo but when she saw the Sistine Chapel she was speechless, as her eyes very slowly swept first over the ceiling and then around the walls. 'Do you know Jill, I have never felt so inspired in all my life and would be quite happy to spend the whole day in here,' she said with feeling.

'There are lots more wonderful things in store Mel, this is only the beginning,' Jill told her, and after the Sistine Chapel they took the lift up to the Dome. The last lap was a flight of narrow, steep dark stairs which took them to the very top from where the views over Rome were breathtaking. They had all their meals sitting outside in the warm sunshine at one of the many pavement cafés, watching the world go by as they ate, and drank the cold, crisp Italian wine. They were chatted up many times by so many hunks with little knowledge of the English language, but the intention quite obvious from their admiring glances. They resisted the temptation but it did their self-confidence a power of good and made them feel very desirable and feminine. They were now able to spend real time on themselves, their dress and make-up, instead of a rush job and wearing mainly uniform which they had done for the previous three and a half months.

There was so much to do and so little time to do it

in but Jill knew the most important sites, which meant they managed to visit the Colosseum, Trevi fountain, the catacombs, the Forum Boarium with a wealth of archae- ological remains, the Spanish steps and so many basilicas that Amelia lost count. They wandered through a lovely park, which was very central, and were accosted by aggressive gypsy children begging for money who, when refused, resorted to spitting at them. The parents of these children kept discreetly out of the way in the bushes and when one of their frightened victims handed over money the parents would suddenly appear and pocket it! This was very frightening so they gave up on the parks after being advised by an Italian lady who had watched the little drama unfold. She told them the gypsies only targeted holidaymakers who they could instinctively pick out. Not only in the park but also along busy streets with expensive shops there were gypsy women squatting on the pavement with a child in their arms and their hands stretched out for money. As people approached the woman would slyly pinch the little soul, making it cry pitifully and the unsuspecting passer-by would hand over money, feeling sorry for the starving child they thought she was holding. In fact the child was extremely well fed and more than used to the painful pinches.

These were the only aspects of Rome that the girls found distasteful and upsetting to their gentle natures. The icing on the cake was on Sunday when they once again visited the Vatican. They had been told the Pope was going to appear on the balcony for prayers and to bless the thousands of pilgrims in the square below. The atmosphere was one of peace and calm with only the sounds of traffic in the distance as this very holy man delivered his blessings. It was all very touching, especially to see nuns and ordinary people in the street – many of whom had travelled hundreds or thousands of miles for just this very spectacle which would be for them a once in a lifetime experience – reduced to tears of joy. They had crammed in so much, thanks to Jill's expert knowledge, that the returning coach journey found the girls gently snoozing in between restaurant stops, tired but very happy!

They arrived back in the village with only a few days to go before departing for England – Amelia to Gatwick and Jill to Manchester. Amelia went and said her goodbyes to Franz and the girls in the tourist office, told them how much she was looking forward to the summer season and thanked them for all their help during the winter. They were sorry to see her leave but assured her they would be there to help if it was needed in the summer, and how they too looked forward to her return. At the Konditorei, as she was chatting to Georg and Gretl, Marcus appeared. There was no denying the delight on his face as he caught sight of Amelia and even though she had just had a coffee she accepted his invitation to another as he sat down at her table.

Gretl went to get their coffees with a slight frown on her face. She was very fond of Amelia and disturbed to see there was still this chemistry between the couple, as she knew it would only lead to unhappiness. Amelia excitedly told him of her trip to Rome but he did not seem particularly interested. All he really wanted to know was when she was coming back. She looked at his handsome face and saw in his eyes a look of extreme tenderness, and suddenly there was a red light flashing somewhere inside her head.

'I will be back early May to attend the seminar at Seefeld and as far as I can see it is going to be a busy summer with trips out every day. It will be interesting for me to see the difference between the winter and summer seasons, not only weather-wise but because unlike the winter where I was in Bachl most of the time, the summer means that

I shall be taking excursions out every day,' she said, her face a picture of happiness and anticipation.

'I hope you will let me show you some of the interesting things in and around Bachl which you would not find on your own, but that I know you would enjoy,' he said hopefully.

'That's very kind of you Marcus but what will Leni think of that?'

There, it was out, and she could have bitten her tongue the moment the words left her lips. He looked like he had been struck, and his face darkened as he said angrily, 'Leni is an old friend of mine and of my whole family. She has been coming here for years and always stays with us as a paying guest the same as the rest. So what does it matter what she would think? I have merely offered to show you around, not proposed marriage!'

Amelia felt extremely foolish and knew she had overstepped the mark. She apologised, saying she must have misunderstood the situation and, anxious to regain his friendship, told him she would be delighted for him to show her around as long as there were no strings. A big smile crossed his face and even though Gretl could not hear what was being said, there was no mistaking the expression on his face – it was one of triumph. Her heart sank.

19

All packed and ready to go, Amelia was picked up by Anne-Marie, as they were going to be on the same flight. Several of the reps had opted for this later flight, which had also given them the opportunity to meet and catch up with their latest news. At Gatwick they lost sight of each other in the frantic rush for the baggage reclaim at the carousel, but all knowing they would be meeting up again very soon. Amelia caught the train to Exeter and was met by her overjoyed parents. They were both astonished to see this beautiful bronzed creature walk towards them, before realising it was their beloved daughter. She was the picture of health and happiness and hugged them both tightly. Her mum's first words were how could she have such a wonderful tan after being in the snow all winter? Amelia laughed and told them she would give them a full account over a nice cup of tea. Once home she chatted nineteen to the dozen about the Tirol and her visit to Rome. Her parents listened enthralled, and were tickled to hear her say that the only thing – apart from themselves and her friends – that she missed was a nice cuppa, as in Austria a cup of tea was a tea bag on a piece of string. It was very weak and looked like cat's pee, which is why a big box of PG Tips was top of her list to take back!

She was the star attraction in the local pub that all her friends frequented. They too had been amazed by the change in her. Whereas she had always been very pretty she was now a bronzed glowing beauty, bubbling over with happiness as she told them all about the winter – except she made no mention of Marcus and Luc. This did not escape their notice – the fact that no man was mentioned in her account of the ski season. 'Did you meet anyone special Mel?' one of her best friends asked. They were all agog waiting for the answer and were disappointed by her negative reply. The girls of the group were not convinced by Amelia's excuse about not having any time to bother with boyfriends. Female intuition told them differently, but if Mel didn't want to tell them, then so be it.

As an afterthought she said, 'Oh, by the way how is that two-timing Alex and his bike?' They all laughed at that and said he was fine but the bike had taken off with another victim and Alex had recently been hanging around with a girl from his office.

The few short weeks she was home were spent on shopping jaunts and trips to the coast with her mother, together with helping to get the hotel ready for the summer. She loved her mother's company more than anyone's; they had a great rapport and were more like sisters. Eileen loved a joke and, like her daughter, had a great sense of humour. Amelia had missed her dreadfully when she was away and was looking forward to spending a few weeks together.

20

At the beginning of May Amelia returned to Bachl. The snow had disappeared and the fields were a mass of wild flowers of many different hues. There were trees abundant with blossom of cherry, plum, apple, pear, mayflower and apricot in the farmers' fields, many of which had been novice ski runs in the winter. There was the constant uplifting sound of cowbells tinkling from the lush green meadows and sunlight sparkled on crystal clear rivers. It seemed even the fir trees with their branches spread out were rejoicing in the summer after being burdened down with snow for months. It was a picture of not only great beauty but also peace and contentment. She was the first of the reps to arrive, as she wanted to research more thoroughly the places of her forthcoming excursions. It filled her with happiness to be back in her lovely flat and to see the locals again and even though she might deny it to others she was rather looking forward to seeing Marcus again – but on a platonic basis!

She didn't have to wait long as, when walking towards the Jagerhof, she could see him waving to her from the balcony. He was sitting with several others and gestured for her to join them. As she approached he got up, pulled out a chair for her and gave her a kiss on the cheek. 'It's good to have you back *Millilein*,' he said, grinning and obviously testing the waters. Amelia tried to ignore the kiss and responded to the questions being asked her from all directions. Yes, she had had a great time and, despite them believing that it always rained in England, assured them it had been absolutely glorious with lots of blossoms and flowers, just like Bachl. One cheekily asked if she had someone special there and all ears pricked up, especially Marcus's waiting for the answer which was 'Yes' and then a deliberate pause before she said, 'My mother.' Marcus looked relieved but the others were disappointed as they thought they were going to hear something exciting. 'That will teach you for being so nosy,' she said tapping the tip of her nose. Marcus's kiss had not gone unnoticed but they all knew better than to rub him up the wrong way so wisely kept schtumm.

When asked which excursions she would be taking, Amelia replied Mayrhofen and the Hintertux glacier, Salzburg, Innsbruck and Italy, Krimml waterfalls and lastly Rattenberg and Lake Achensee with one more to find but it must only be a half-day trip. 'Any suggestions?' she asked, looking around the table and getting a lot of good ideas. 'Hang on a moment chaps while I write these down.' She scrambled for her notepad in her briefcase. Marcus hadn't said a word but looked very thoughtful.

'I know a very interesting place to take Brits, that no other reps know about and which would be special to them,' he said earnestly, and then added, 'I have a book at home with all the details, I'll go and get it.' He was gone before Amelia had a chance to ask him to enlarge on it. He reappeared a few minutes later armed with the mysterious book and to the chagrin of his chums insisted Amelia joined him at another table out of earshot, before he would disclose where this secret place was. He opened the book to a page depicting a very old castle and explained it was called Castle Friedberg, which was owned by Count Von Trapp, a cousin of the Salzburg Von Trapps, and where the family had frequently spent holidays. Amelia's ears immediately pricked up, he had her full attention as he explained it was situated in the Inn Valley near Schwaz and if she could make time he would take her there. The Count would only allow small coach parties, which is why the tour operators did not know of it.

'I'm sure if you went and met him he would be charmed, perhaps in allowing you to take a larger coach. It would certainly be well worth a try, what do you think *Millilein?*' Amelia was dumbstruck with a thousand different things running through her head. Apart from The Sound of Music being the most wonderful inspiring musical she had ever seen, the Count and the castle sounded intriguing and would be one hell of an addition to her excursion plan!

'Marcus I am going to take you up on that offer. When are you free? I have over a week before I go to Seefeld,' she said excitedly.

Marcus hadn't known what her reaction would be when he suggested Friedberg as she had so often cold-shouldered him, but she was visibly very eager to know more and to visit the castle. He felt very pleased with himself as he walked home whistling after arranging to take his *Millilein* to Castle Friedberg the following day.

As good as his promise he picked her up from her flat at ten o'clock and was in high spirits and overjoyed at the thought of actually doing something to please *Millilein*. Just after Schwaz in the Inn Valley he took a left turn and headed towards the densely wooded mountain area. He pointed out the castle, which was, unlike a lot of the other castles, not too far up the mountain. He parked the car and held her hand as they climbed the rugged slope leading up to the castle. It was nestled in the trees in an idyllic setting. There were huge old wooden double doors with a quaint ring-pull bell. It all seemed surreal as she could hear it ding-dinging from somewhere behind the doors. It was so quiet there with only the sound of birdsong, until suddenly a little door that was set into one of the big ones slowly opened and there standing in front of them was a wizened old man with a very brown face and goatee beard. Marcus politely asked if it was possible he could show his friend the castle.

'Better than that, I will give you a guided tour! Allow me to introduce myself. Count Von Trapp,' he said, firstly shaking Amelia's hand and then on to Marcus. They had a lovely conversation with the old man, who obviously enjoyed company and told them the history of the castle. When she thought the moment was right and after spending over an hour with this charming gentleman Amelia said, 'Count, I hope you don't think I'm being impertinent but I am a rep and I would love to bring a group of my people here to see this wonderful historical castle. Could I possibly have your permission to come once a week?'

'It all depends, my dear, on how many people,' was his reply.

'Well our coach has a capacity of 56 but after seeing the size of the castle and taking into account that not everyone would be able to cope with the steep slope I would limit it to 30,' she said with more than a trace of hope in her voice.

'If you would promise me that 30 would be the absolute maximum and you would let me know a day in advance of the numbers to expect, I think I could agree to that. I only allow one coach party a day as I myself do the guided tour. There will be an entrance fee of 15 schillings with the tour included of course.'

Amelia was overjoyed, vigorously shook his hand and made a provisional booking for the first visit which according to her diary would be the twenty-seventh of May at 10 am.

After making many notes and promising to phone the numbers through the day before, they exited the big old doors and stepped out into the bright sunlight over the Inn Valley.

'My God Marcus, this is an unbelievable scoop! I know my guests will be as enthusiastic as me at the prospect of visiting a Von Trapp family castle and I just know it is going to be a very popular excursion. I can't wait to tell the other reps!'

'Good, good, I had a feeling you would be inspired and I'm happy I was able to help.'

'Marcus please let me treat you to lunch as a mark of my gratitude, I would love to go to Wienerwald again and I don't think it is very far away.'

'No *Millilein*, it is not far and that would be a very good idea but there is no way I would allow you to pay. But perhaps I can think of something else you can reward me with!' Seeing the shock and disbelief of what she had just heard on her face, Marcus quickly said, 'That was a joke Milli, I was teasing you but it was worth it just to see the look on your face!' He almost doubled up with laughter. Fortunately for him, Milli too saw the funny side of it, but for a few short moments she had contemplated jumping out of the car!

She had noticed the Swarovski crystal factory was only a short distance away and pointing it out said, 'Do we have time for a very quick visit as this would make it a really interesting excursion if I could incorporate a visit there after we left the castle?' He nodded and drove into the huge parking area. She didn't know what she was expecting but the sight before her was dazzling and vast with everything from jewellery to carriage clocks and chandeliers. The price for each item was displayed in German, Italian, French and English currency. Knowing how expensive Swarovski was in the UK Amelia realised the prices direct from the factory were distinctly cheaper. She was directed into the office and after a chat with a very accommodating sales manager had arranged a visit with her group on the twenty-seventh and afterwards on a regular basis until late September. Feeling very pleased with herself she gave Marcus – who had been waiting in the café – a big hug and told him that, thanks to him, she had just organised what she knew would be one of the most popular excursions of the summer.

They had a leisurely lunch with a few glasses of wine, then Marcus suggested that because it was such a lovely day, and as he did not have to rush back, he show her some of the other villages in the area. Still on a high, Amelia was more than up for it. He drove higher up the valley through dense forest and suddenly there was a meadow in front of them with a little village nestling in the middle. She was amazed as, from the valley looking upwards, it seemed there was only a mass of trees leading up to the mountain peaks, and here was a plateau with built-up roads even though narrow. Marcus explained there were a few more plateaus with small villages further up. None of this could be seen from the valley. They stopped and had coffee and gateaux at one of the little cafés and chatted away like old friends quite happy in each other's company. She found Marcus not only amusing but also enthusiastic, telling her about a wealth of local customs and history that she absorbed and made a mental note to add to her information for excursions.

They arrived back in Bachl early evening and before entering her flat Amelia once again thanked him for a really wonderful day and without realising what she was doing kissed him on the cheek. Marcus smiled and said he enjoyed it too, picked up and kissed her hand and, so as not to push his luck, got back in the car and with a wave drove off. She went into her flat, sat down, her head all over the place over the day's events. Trying to push all thoughts of Marcus to the back of her mind, she started to write up the new additions to her already interesting information notes. As far as Marcus was concerned the warning light kept on flashing to green with no amber in between! The next day she went to see Georg with her full list of excursions and together they sorted out the days, destinations and prices of each trip. He was impressed by her enthusiasm and the thoughtfulness she had put into her itinerary, especially the Castle Friedberg trip which he knew the other reps would want to do when they heard what she had accomplished. He also knew there was not much chance of them getting a similar arrangement with the Count unless he changed his mind and allowed afternoon visits.

At the seminar she presented her list of excursions to a very impressed Anne-Marie who remarked how advantageous it had been to Amelia arriving back early in the Tirol to enable her to do so much research into the places on the excursion list. The other reps were keen to copy her notes which she did not mind one little bit as she had picked up quite a lot of tips from them too, so it wasn't such a bad exchange! The hotel put on a super evening meal for them and afterwards they all sat in the bar chatting nineteen to the dozen, it was like one big happy family. Remembering her promise to Luc she asked Anne-Marie if they were free the following evening and explained her reason. The answer was yes but if she was going to forego the evening meal to let the hotel know. This all sorted she rang Luc who said he would pick her up.

After an exhausting day at the seminar she was really looking forward to seeing Luc again. His greeting was warm and friendly and they chatted away during their meal at the fish restaurant. She told him excitedly about the Castle Friedhof trip she had organised for her guests and he was intrigued to know how on earth she had managed to get there from Bachl without a car, as he was aware exactly where it was and knew she would have to make two bus changes and even then have a long walk. It would take the best part of a day to get there and back. He was surprised when she told him her mode of transport and with whom. Amelia saw the frown and questioning look appear on his face and said, perhaps a bit too quickly, 'He's quite a nice person when you get to know him. I think perhaps I judged him too harshly by listening to hearsay.'

Lucien told her to be careful as he knew all about these ski instructors and the broken hearts they leave behind.

'Luc, he is a good friend and that is what he will remain, I am a big girl now and my rose-tinted spectacles flew off a while back, you can believe me!'

Not one to pry, he changed the subject but was nonetheless concerned as he was very fond of this particular English rose. After a lovely evening he drove her back to the hotel and before she left told her that in Summer he spent the weekends up at his mountain chalet so would not be visiting Bachl very often. He explained that he made the most of the summer months there, as due to the snowdrifts it was unapproachable in winter.

'Tell you what Amelia, if the weather is still good at the end of September I will take you up there before you go back to England, but please ring me anytime when you are in Innsbruck as you know I love your company,' he said sincerely. He opened the car door and towered over her as he shook her hand and kissed her cheek, 'Don't forget!' he said as he drove off.

Amelia didn't know just what to think but felt very flattered that in the space of a week two handsome men had kissed her cheek. The rest of the reps were still in the bar and beckoned her over, all dying to know who the gorgeous hunk with the Mercedes sports car was, but they were disappointed when told he was an old friend!

The next few days were so busy with so much to cram in that she never really had time to think about either Marcus or Luc. She arrived back in Bachl, her arms full with her summer uniform, masses of paperwork, and the sleeves for the summer brochures, and was delighted to find a message from Jill – who had arrived back while she had been at the seminar – to meet up in the Jagerhof at seven, as she had some exciting news to tell her.

When she arrived, all the summer reps were already there and together they compared notes and organised who was going where for the excursions and evening entertainment. After all this was sorted out Jill took Amelia out onto the balcony and, brimming over with excitement, told her that she had met this smashing chap quite by chance whilst on her month's break. He was an archaeologist and one of a party on a dig at some Roman settlements near her home in Colwyn Bay. They had met in the local library where he was doing some research and had asked her if she was from the area. On hearing she was Colwyn Bay born and bred he asked her for some information about the area. He was tall, dark, and very attractive with a wicked sense of humour, and from London. They had just clicked and Jill had spent almost her entire holiday in his company.

This accounted for the change Amelia noticed in her at the meeting with the reps. She appeared to be different but in a happy sort of way and it had been noticeable that she was not concentrating on whatever was being discussed but drifting off with a little smile on her face. Amelia listened enthralled, she had never seen Jill in this light before even though she had ample opportunities but had never taken any particular interest in men – a 'typical career woman', as Amelia had wrongly thought. Her whole face had lit up as she was telling Amelia about this Richard, and looking at her pretty freckled face, blonde shoulder-length curly hair and lithe figure, Amelia could quite see how Edward had been bowled over. 'He's coming for two weeks in July Mel, and I can't wait for you to meet him,' she said breathlessly.

Amelia was really amused by this total change in one of her favourite friends and was very happy for her. 'Now tell me what *you* have been up to!' Jill said almost as an afterthought. 'What's the latest with Marcus and Lucien?' Amelia didn't know where to start but casually told her of the castle and also the meeting with Luc – but it seemed to pale in comparison to Jill's news.

21

There were only a few days to go before the first guests arrived and Amelia was more than ready and very pleased with her information books for the hotels. After delivering them she was walking through the village when Marcus pulled up in his car. 'Hello *Millilein*, I am going up to the Moser farmhouse to do a fitting, do you fancy a ride?' he said cheerfully. Her first reaction was to refuse, but she didn't, as she would have loved to see the inside of a really old farmhouse and also, even though she would not admit it, was glad to see him. She hopped in and off they went up the mountain, both happy in each other's company.

Simon and Moidl were delighted to see them and after the fitting the Schnapps and beer were brought out. Moidl told her the Schnapps was a new batch that had only been distilled the previous week and seeing Amelia's interest offered to show her the Still in the cellar. It all seemed antiquated but obviously very efficient. She already knew that every farmhouse had a still and the Schnapps was made mainly from apples and pears, but to actually see it drip, drip into the containers was an eye-opener and she felt she would get drunk from the strong fumes without even touching a drop! Moidl then took her into the kitchen where fresh bread had just been baked and offered her a slice with their home cured Speck – a bacon that had been smoked over an open fire for weeks. It was delicious.

As they sat in the living room the children appeared, all nine of them, of ages ranging from two to seventeen. The eldest three produced a guitar, squeezebox and harp, then played while the younger ones entertained them with dancing and singing. It was spellbinding and had more than a touch of The Sound of Music about it. It gave Amelia an idea for the spare night she had left for evening entertainment, which she originally had planned for a mystery trip.

'Moidl, what would you and Simon think of me bringing my guests up to see an original farmhouse, and eat home-made bread and home-cured ham washed down with home-made Schnapps?' she said enthusiastically. Moidl looked puzzled until Amelia explained that if she would consider this she would not only delight her guests but would make a nice profit to swell the family's meagre income. Simon said it was a very good idea but they had to talk about it. 'Oh, please do, I promise my guests are well behaved and would really appreciate to see something original and not commercialised. I know they would be as inspired as I am,' she pleaded.

Moidl looked at Simon and said it was worth a try but first let's work out what the guests would expect. Amelia replied exactly what she had been given – a thick slice of bread with ham and a glass of Schnapps. Any beer would be paid for separately.

'You do realise Milli the most we could accommodate in one go would be twenty-six and limited to just the one night of the week? Then let's see how we go, but I must stipulate we would not even consider any of the other reps and their guests, we know all about holidaymakers who can't hold their drink! This is purely because we know and trust you.'

They all got their heads together and came up with the inclusive charge to each guest on the understanding that it would be the same night every week and that Amelia gave them 24 hours' notice of how many to expect.

Elated, and without even noticing, she allowed Marcus's arm to creep around her shoulder as he led her to the car. He had been impressed by the way she had charmed Simon and Moidl into opening their house to the public and knew she would make a success of it. The kids too had been excited and had joined in with the enthusiasm of their parents at the thought of playing and dancing for a crowd of English people, not to mention the added bonus of having some extra income! '*Millilein*, you never cease to amaze me,' he said adoringly.

'Actually Marcus it is because of you that I have two exclusive and exciting trips for my guests and I really appreciate this, not to mention enjoying your company while these successful transactions have taken place.'

They looked at each other as if to say 'and what now?' Before he could say anything Amelia blurted out, 'I am very fond of you and you have become someone special to me but you know it can go no further.'

'*Millilein*, I have loved you from the first time I saw you stumbling out of the kitchen when you took a wrong turn at the Jagerhof over a year ago. It does not matter to me if you do not feel the same but I can wait. Meanwhile I hope we can remain as we are now,' he replied with great feeling in his voice.

'If that is enough for you, dear Marcus, then so be it,' she replied with tenderness.

She asked to be dropped off in the village centre as she had some more work to do at the tourist office. She put her hand over his, looked into his beautiful smiling eyes, gave a smile, got out and entered the tourist office, to meet a surprised Jill who had seen it all. Not only Jill, but Franz, Heidi and Anna all looking questioningly at one another!

Once outside, Amelia knew exactly what Jill was going to say. 'What's going on Mel? I couldn't help but notice the way you and Marcus looked at each other. I don't have to be a rocket scientist to see there is something far deeper than a platonic friendship between you two?' Amelia tried to explain her thoughts and feelings and obviously needed someone close to give her some help and advice. Only Jill fitted into that category. 'Mel, take things easy, you are treading on dangerous ground as far as Marcus is concerned. You are well aware of his history and at the age of twenty-nine he is not likely to change his ways permanently. I know how you have felt for a long time but it seems to have got to a stage now where there is gossip and anticipation in the village over you both. I really do not want to see you hurt.'

'Jill, Jill, nothing has gone beyond the friendship stage. I admit I have feelings for him but they are completely under control. I vowed after Alex that no man would ever have the chance to break my heart again and I meant it,' she said very convincingly.

'What about Lucien? Where does he fit into the frame? He intrigues me, but how on earth he has got to 30 without ever marrying beats me. I think you must have a penchant for older men and they certainly seem taken with you!'

Amelia replied that Lucien had girl friends, was charming, she loved his company as he made her laugh and treated her like a lady, but she had no romantic interest in him nor he with her – theirs was a platonic friendship with no strings. 'In fact the last thing I want is an involvement with Luc as it would probably spoil a beautiful friendship!' she sincerely told her friend.

'Well there's one good thing about the summer season as far as work is concerned, that's the fact that with so many excursions and evening entertainment we have little

free time and that does not bode well with a romance!'
Jill said with a laugh and arm in arm they went for a
walk down the valley where they were waved at by Elsa
who ran the post office and who was sitting outside her
pretty little chalet. She called to the girls to come and
join her, and once seated on the bench outside her front
door she reached up and picked them an apricot each
from the tree that framed her door. They were warm
from the sun and had a completely different flavour from
the ones they were used to from the supermarkets back
home. This was one of the many things that endeared
them to Bachl, this complete acceptance and friendship
from the villagers, and they loved it.

22

Airport day arrived, with Amelia clad in her stunning summer uniform consisting of turquoise suit, white blouse and turquoise cravat. The summer guests were from quite a mixed age group but no teenage and twenty-something ravers as the ski crowd had been. These were more sightseers and early to bed and early to rise people who listened intently as she introduced herself and the coach driver and welcomed them to Austria. She explained that once they were free of the airport and on the autobahn she would tell them a little about the country and its customs.

Once on the autobahn she broke the silence by pointing to a huge billboard where in enormous letters was written *GUTE FAHRT* and proceeded to tell them they could say that as often as they liked as it meant 'Have a good trip', 'so I hope you all have a *Gute Fahrt*!' There were smiles and giggles amongst her passengers. 'Something else I must point out to you and that is every bakery and café in the Tirol will have a fantastic choice of goodies and in amongst these you will find Krapfen which are the Austrian equivalent of our doughnuts.' She finished by telling them to try a Krapfen on one of their Ausfahrts. By now the whole coach, including Heinz the driver, were in fits of laughter. Once they had all calmed down she pointed out one of the many farmhouses they passed and explained they all had a huge bell on the roof which was used as a means of communication to other farmhouses and the workers in the fields to call them in for their meals. They had different peals – like the Morse code – which enabled them to ring out messages such as births, deaths or if they needed help. There were no phones in those days and this was their means of communication, but since the introduction of phones they are now merely ornamental and even the new farmhouses that are built will still have a bell on the top purely for ornamental purposes. She told them about their hotels and meal times and advised them to use the public phone boxes rather than the hotel phones as it was significantly cheaper, they were circled in red on the maps she had given them, together with the doctor's surgery.

Amelia went on to give in great detail the excursions and evening entertainment available to them which was also on the information sheets they had been given. She finished by telling them the time of the welcome meeting the next morning, where they could ask questions and book up any of the excursions or evening entertainment and where she would give out more maps of the many walks in and around Bachl. Appreciating they must be tired, she said she was putting on a James Last tape of classics for them to relax to until they reached the Bavarian/Austrian border where their passports would be checked. Afterwards it would only take an hour before they were in Bachl. It was so completely different from the winter as not only was there no ski school involved but no après ski sessions either. As they approached the village she suggested her guests unwind in their hotels before their meal and as it was such a lovely day perhaps it would be a good opportunity to get their maps out and familiarise themselves with the village. She pointed out the Jagerhof where she held her 'office hours' between six and seven every evening to book up any of the guests who had already decided what they wanted to do, which would ease the flow at the welcome meeting the next morning.

The first excursion was for Sunday afternoon. It was *Fahrt ins Blau* which translated into Mystery Trip and was fully booked. On this her first summer trip Amelia learnt a valuable addition to her already informative notes on each trip. This took the form of being asked at each stop they made where the nearest loo was. Consequently, she made a point of not only finding the location but also whether it was free or how much it cost on every stop they made for each of her trips out. This was going to be a bonus for her guests as it saved them the embarrassment of having to ask, as she informed them over the mike. If the loo was in sight she pointed it out or if not could tell them exactly where to find it. This was very much appreciated by all her guests, especially those in the upper age bracket!

The reps decided they would have to have their meetings on Saturday evenings after their office hours as it was the only time free, the rest being taken up with excursions and evening entertainment. A few weeks into the season Amelia casually told them what a boon it had been to her guests knowing the location of the loos. They thought this was hilarious especially as she had said it so seriously, but their ears had pricked up and they eagerly took notes of Amelia's important findings! Sue sat there with a smile on her face and said, 'Do you know Mel, you never cease to amaze me. You could write a book about your experiences in the Tirol and call it Tirolu!' This really tickled the girls, and her nickname of Tirolu was created.

Every week she was fortunate to have lovely, appreciative guests. Sometimes she would have single people on their own because of bereavement, divorce, having no one to travel with or just because they preferred it that way. One week a young woman with a two-year-old little boy arrived.

She was very quiet and withdrawn, dressed in beautiful clothes and booked into the most expensive hotel. She did not turn up for the information meeting or the office hours, so Amelia asked her guests staying in the same hotel if they had seen her. They replied that she had been at breakfast and evening dinner but kept herself and the little boy apart from them. On hearing this, Amelia decided to visit her at the hotel but found from the receptionist that the little boy was put into the nursery every day while the mother went off on her own. She reluctantly added that when the woman arrived back at the hotel she appeared to be the worse for drink, and the staff were quite concerned as the child had been left in the bedroom in the evenings while she sat on her own in the bar or in the nightclub. Amelia told the receptionist that she would be back after her excursion and would have a talk with the woman.

True to her word, she arrived back at the hotel before she had her office hours and was told that the guest was in her room and had appeared once again worse for wear. She tapped on the bedroom door and was aware of the child crying inside. Despite tapping more loudly, his mother would not answer the door. Afraid that something had happened to her Amelia went quickly to get the manager who brought the pass key and let her in. The tot was sitting at the foot of the bed tugging at the foot of his prostrate mother. Amelia scooped him up into her arms to try and comfort him while the manager shook his mother's shoulder. There was a strong smell of alcohol about her and she was absolutely flat out. Hans the manager suggested he took the little boy to his wife to look after and let Mrs Allen sleep it off. Amelia said she would have to arrange to merge her guests with another reps' for the evening entertainment and would be right back after her office hours. She said she would leave a note for Mrs Allen to let her know where her son was just in case she awoke before she got back. Hans agreed with this decision and emphasised that the hotel was not prepared to put up with this behaviour and that all the staff were worried about the child. 'Leave it to me Hans, I will let Mrs Allen know in no uncertain terms that unless she pulls herself together she will be on the next flight home.'

As soon as her office hours were over and after explaining to Jill the circumstances and arranging for her to take over her guests, Amelia quickly made her way back to the Alpenruhe. Hans accompanied her to Mrs Allen's bedroom to find that she was still fast asleep. Amelia gently shook her shoulder, at the same time calling her name, and after several attempts she appeared to stir. Her eyes were bloodshot and watery and had dark shadows underneath. She looked startled and for a moment didn't know where she was. She sat bolt upright and with her eyes darting around the room cried, 'Where's my baby?!'

'It's all right Mrs Allen, he is in safe hands, only we were very concerned when we could not wake you a few hours ago and your little boy was in a very distressed state.' Hans excused himself and left Amelia alone to talk to her. She could not help but feel sorry for Mrs Allen, as it was obvious this poor soul was in need of help. It soon became obvious why she was in such distress as she sobbed her heart out telling Amelia how after only four years of marriage her husband had run off with her best friend. She had loved and still loved him very much and had no idea they had been carrying on. She had lots of support from her family and friends but after the hurt and humiliation, not to mention the heartbreak, she had suddenly decided she had to get away. After assuring her parents she was all right but needed a break, she had booked this holiday, thinking she could clear her head, but it had the reverse effect. Instead of giving her son her full attention and hoping to unwind she had been overcome with the whole reality of the situation and had never felt so lonely or unloved in her life. She was in a foreign country with none of her friends or family to support her. She had found solace in a bottle of wine the first night of the holiday and, not being used to drinking except for the odd glass, found this was the only way she could blot out her sadness. Tom, her son, had become very clingy and much as she loved him she found she could not help herself whilst sober, despite the guilt she felt for not caring and looking after him as she should have.

Amelia listened sympathetically and found herself protectively putting her arm around this sobbing woman's shoulder. 'There is no man worth all this heartbreak. You are a very attractive woman with a beautiful healthy little boy and for his sake and yours you have to look after yourself. The answer is not in a bottle but counting your blessings of which there must be many. He is obviously not worthy of you so, instead of going under, surprise him by coming out on top! Pick yourself up, get your make-up on and face the world, you have done nothing wrong. Think positive, please? That little tot needs the loving caring mother he had a short while ago, he must be very frightened and confused, Mrs Allen.'

'Please call me Jo, and thank you Amelia. With your words of wisdom you have begun to put things in perspective, you are a very kind person and I promise you this stupid boozing phase is now a thing of the past. Please forgive me and thank you so much for your help. You have no idea how good it feels being able to talk about it to someone outside the family.'

'Jo, I would like you and Tom to join us for the excursion tomorrow to Rattenberg and Achensee. It is not a long trip and Tom would love to see the lake and the boats.

There is plenty of space for him to run around there, and if you like I will take you to a farmhouse where they have chickens, ducks, pigs and goats.'

'That would be great Amelia and thank you, I feel better already.'

After reuniting mother with son, Amelia went back to the Jagerhof, feeling so relieved that what could have been a very sad situation where she had to involve Anne-Marie was now diffused. She could still remember the shock, hurt and humiliation she had felt at Alex's betrayal, but at least she had not been married to him let alone with a baby, so what that poor woman must have gone through didn't bear thinking about. It certainly made her very sympathetic to her cause and any way she could help Jo and her little boy, she would.

The rest of the week went smoothly with Jo and Tom becoming part of the group, and the tot was made a fuss of by the other guests. Apart from the odd occasion when she appeared a little wistful, Jo seemed to be coping very well and surprised Amelia when she asked if it was possible for her to stay on for another week as it was doing herself and Tom the power of good. It would give her more breathing space before going home and picking up the pieces. After several phone calls and a bit of organising this was arranged, even to the point that they could keep the same bedroom.

Amelia hadn't seen much of Marcus all week, in fact she had not seen him at all and feeling a little concerned asked Maria the waitress if she had seen him. She was told that he was working as he had a lot of orders due to a big wedding in a few weeks' time in Rattenberg, so he had been busy almost around the clock. That's good news, thought Amelia, at least it must have curbed his drinking, but she missed seeing his cheeky grin and having the odd conversation with him.

At the next reps' meeting it was arranged for the bowling night to be changed to Thursday as the village brass band played in the square on Friday evenings throughout the summer. They all informed their guests about the change the following week and told them to make sure they got there early as the band paraded around the centre of the village before taking their positions outside the church, weather permitting. They played all sorts of lovely music from marches to favourites from musicals. The reps bagged a table outside the Jagerhof and sat back and relaxed whilst enjoying the music, wine and each other's company.

The band looked so smart and impressive in their colourful uniforms, and Amelia's eyes were trained on one musician in particular – Marcus! She felt a sense of pride and joy and could not deny she still had feelings for him, especially when his beautiful eyes spotted her on the balcony and his face lit up. It was the practice for the band to all pour into the Jagerhof after the concert, and instead of joining the rest in the bar, Marcus drew a chair up next to her, greeted her friends and pointedly asked how she was and how she was coping with the summer season.

'It's great Marcus, just great,' she replied.

'I've heard you are doing a grand job. It's just a pity you are so tied up as I wanted to take you up to the Grundl Alm, but being as it's a good two-hour walk up the mountain that would not be possible with your workload, which is a pity because you would love it!' he said, with not much hope.

She had heard about the Alm which was where the farmer and his son from the Grundlhof farm took their cows up to higher pastures in the summer. They had a hut there where they stayed all summer. It was directly above the farmhouse and had a winch that transported the milk down every day and also brought up fresh food, beer and Schnapps. It was a favourite walk for the hikers and also very popular with the locals. They supplied bread, cheese, smoked ham – which they cured themselves – beer and Schnapps. This provided them with an extra income and was a big attraction.

'I would have loved a visit there, Marcus, but unless I can arrange with one of the reps to take one of my morning excursions I'm afraid it won't be a possibility,' she replied.

The girls were listening to this exchange and Jill quickly offered to take over her Friedberg trip, after seeing the hope in her friend's face. She knew it was pointless trying to shield Amelia from the attentions of Marcus as it was quite obvious she had meant that she wanted to go. Besides, Jill was dying to do the Friedberg excursion and perhaps after talking with the Count he might allow her to bring her group too! There was no disguising the delight on Marcus and Amelia's faces and they arranged for the trek up to the Grundl Alm for the week after next, as Marcus was still up to his eyes with the wedding outfits.

They stayed and chatted long after the reps had moved on to the nightclub, and were joined by several of the band once the seats were vacated. The squeezebox and guitar were produced and an impromptu singsong followed. They were joined by many of the British guests from inside when they heard the music. The rascal Koni encouraged them to sing 'Clementine' which was a firm favourite with the village boys who only knew the English words of the chorus but could play the whole melody. The guests obliged but when it came to the verse which had the words 'a splinter in her foot' the boys all clapped and fell about laughing! The bewildered guests laughed too but had no idea that splinter was the same word in

German as English, but 'foot' was another thing altogether. In dialect 'foot' means a woman's private parts! Amelia had already come across this and had it explained to her by Traudl the previous winter when she too had been puzzled by the response. The Brits would never know what had caused the hilarity – they just assumed the boys had a funny sense of humour at Clementine having a splinter in her foot! After a lovely evening Amelia reluctantly said her goodnights and walked up the road feeling extremely happy.

She had let Lucien know about the change to the Innsbruck/Italy trip and on the Thursday he was there to meet the coach as it pulled in. They went once again to the Hopfgarten restaurant, had a meal with wine and talked and talked. Well, mostly Amelia talked, telling an attentive Luc all about what she had been up to – without once ever referring to Marcus. He listened and looked very amused. When asked about how his life had been since she last saw him he seemed a bit evasive. Sensing this, Amelia asked if all was well with his girlfriend and business but immediately wished she hadn't as his face visibly darkened. 'Just a few little problems that can easily be sorted,' he replied.

Amelia was not convinced but there was no way she was going to pursue this line of conversation, especially as it was quite obvious he had no intention of elaborating on his problems. Instead, she suggested a walk around the park before she had to join the coach. Arm in arm like old friends they wandered around the beautiful gardens and sat for a few minutes in the shade as it was so hot.

'I might come up to Bachl at the weekend so I can stretch my legs and also get away from the dust and humidity of the town,' he said out of the blue.

'I look forward to seeing you Luc. Are you giving your mountain chalet a miss?' she asked innocently but once again his face had darkened as he replied, 'Yes, I feel like a change!' and that was the abrupt end of the conversation.

On Saturday, Jo Allen and her son Tom sat at the front of the coach pointing out various sights they were passing. This was a completely different woman than the one who had arrived two weeks ago so distressed, thought Amelia. She felt comfortable with the knowledge that this break had given Jo time to collect her thoughts and prepare her for the obviously difficult and stressful time she had ahead. At the airport, Jo gave her a big hug and thanked her yet again for being so kind and thoughtful. 'You have no idea how much this holiday has done for me, and thanks to your words of wisdom I really feel my batteries have been charged and that I can now face the future – whatever might be thrown at me!' said a tearful Jo.

'Please write and tell me how you are as I shall be thinking of you both,' said a very sincere Amelia.

23

The new arrivals were once again a nice crowd and included a young married couple with Ellie their pretty little two-year-old daughter. They were quite happy staying in the village during the day either going for long walks or visiting the swimming pool. They turned up for nearly every one of Amelia's office hours and thoroughly enjoyed themselves. Little Ellie chatted away telling her with great delight what she had seen and done during the day. 'She has taken a liking to you and asks every day when she is going to see "Melia" again,' said Anne her mother. Amelia had always loved kids and had the knack of coming down to their level instead of expecting them to come up to hers. Ellie was no exception, and at the office hours would make a beeline for her lap.

On the return transfer, after their week-long stay, Anne came down to the front of the bus just as they had entered into the Inn Valley. 'I'm afraid Ellie is feeling sick, do you think she could possibly sit on your lap here at the front as I think it may be due to the movement at the back where we are sitting.'

'That's no problem Anne, plonk her down here,' said Amelia patting her lap. She distracted Ellie's attention by pointing out cows, horses, pigs, and tractors and there were even some hang-gliders. Ellie was quite happy sitting there and seemed to have forgotten all about feeling sick, then barely half an hour from the airport she suddenly *was* sick and a trail of congealed milk and scrambled eggs

151

cascaded over Amelia's jacket and sleeve. She quickly grabbed the tissues and was trying to mop it up while at the same time keeping perfectly calm so as not to upset the little tot who seemed quite unperturbed by it. Ellie didn't cry or make any retching noises so it was only the driver and people sitting in the front seats who knew what had happened. There was absolutely nothing Amelia could do about her suit until she got to the airport but she called Anne to the front to collect the little girl while she tried to sponge the mess with her bottle of mineral water and the tissues. She was still chatting away to Ellie when she was aware of her lap getting warm and realised not only had the tot been sick, she was doing a wee as well!

Anne was very upset when she saw Amelia's suit, and apologised profusely but Amelia told her not to worry, it was an accident and could not be helped. Inwardly she was nearly hysterical thinking about how she was going to be able to greet her new arrivals. When she saw Anne-Marie in the departures hall and explained what had happened it was all taken out of her hands as she was told to go back to her coach and Anne-Marie would meet the arrivals and deliver them to her. Amelia noticed the mirth on the other reps' faces, who also realised 'There but for the grace of God go I!' She couldn't get back to the coach quickly enough and was very conscious of the mottled brown, yellows and white displayed on her beautiful suit. The turquoise was a perfect background to emphasise the dreadful mess and attracted quite a bit of attention as she hurried back to the coach. It was painfully obvious that Heinz the driver thought it hilarious and Amelia knew it would be a focal point of discussion when he got into the Jagerhof on their return.

With her passengers all safely seated she took the microphone, welcomed them and introduced herself and

Heinz. Before she went any further she apologised for her appearance and explained the whole sorry saga but instead of sympathy there were roars of laughter and the ice was broken before she even started on her commentary! The smell of sick and wee wafted up to her nose as the coach became warmer but she was delighted to see Heinz wrinkling up his nose too. 'Touché,' she said, with a satisfied smirk on her face, but knew they both couldn't get the two-hour-plus transfer over quickly enough. Once in the village she got Heinz to drive straight to her flat and apologised once again to the passengers, explaining she would be only a matter of minutes while she had a quick change. Later, there followed an internal fax from Anne-Marie to all reps to advise them to refrain from taking children on their laps should a similar situation occur!

At her office hours Amelia was happy to find she had a really nice crowd of people once again with the exception of one family who seemed a little odd and rather withdrawn. This was obvious the next morning at the welcome meeting when they complained about the evening meal being rubbish. Amelia was really taken aback as the hotel they were in was renowned for the quality and large helpings served to their guests. She asked the other guests at the same hotel if they had enjoyed their evening meal and heard nothing but praise for the delicious goulash they had been served.

Mr White, the head of the family, spoke out and said, 'I don't care what you call it, it was rubbish and we don't eat rubbish at home, my family are used to good tasty satisfying meals not this foreign muck.'

Amelia didn't know how she controlled herself from saying 'and what sort of rubbish are you used to at home?' but after such an onslaught asked what sort of food they were used to so that she could have a word with the manager to try and accommodate them with the appropriate equivalent. She managed to contain herself from laughing when a relieved Mr White said, 'We like sausage and chips or pie and chips or egg and chips or chops and chips – that sort of good wholesome food!'

'Leave it with me and I will sort it for you,' she assured him. After the meeting Amelia went to their hotel and explained the situation to the manager who told her it would be no problem. Well let's hope this will satisfy the family, she thought to herself.

She had not seen Luc and wondered if he had actually come up to the village. She was quite concerned, as he certainly did not seem to be his usual cheerful self when she last saw him, and it was obvious something was worrying him but he had not been prepared to discuss it with her. I'll give him a ring during the week to see if he is all right, she thought, and went to meet Jill at the Jagerhof to discuss the trip Jill was going to cover for her.

While waiting for Jill in the bar she could not help but notice a family of new arrivals – they were all over six feet tall and consisted of a mother and father, their sons who were the spitting image of their father, and the sons' wives. They were quite loud and spoke with 'Hooray Henry' accents. The father went up to the busy bar and started to order in German. Gerda, the owner, told him she could speak English but despite this the man insisted in ordering in German.

'*Zwei grosses Bier, eine weiss Wein, eine rot Wein und* a dry Martini,' he said looking very pleased and rather superior. Gerda had a faint smile on her face and served up the drinks but when it came to the dry Martini she handed him three!

'What's this?' he asked in English.

Pointing at the glasses Gerda replied, '*Ein, zwei, drei Martini*.'

154

'Oh I beg your pardon,' the old gent said, 'but I only wanted one.'

'Then perhaps in future when you order you speak all *Deutsch* or all English,' said Gerda with a smirk, and made him pay for all three. Sportingly he accepted them and joined his family who were all laughing. 'Well that's put me in my place!' he said with a broad smile. All in the bar had noticed this little scenario, including the many locals who had enjoyed Gerda's response to what had appeared at the time a rather rude man.

When Jill arrived, Amelia told her what she had just missed. Jill responded with 'They obviously don't realise there is no class distinction in the village and they don't need to try to impress, but they will soon learn. I've seen this all before.' Between them they got the excursion to Castle Friedberg organised. Jill had misgivings about Amelia's trek up to the Alm with Marcus but knew it was pointless saying anything more than she had already said, especially as her friend was so excited about it.

Jill had been right about the tall family, as when she was next in the Jagerhof bar after her office hours they were there again but with none of the loudness and high-falluting attitude. Instead they were chatting away to the holidaymakers and seemed to be thoroughly enjoying themselves. Seeing Amelia enter, Tall Father approached her and asked if there was any possibility of six adults joining her coach for the Innsbruck/Italy trip. He explained they had looked at her information book in their hotel, which they were all impressed with, and thought it would be a nice idea, as after driving all the way from London neither of them wanted any more motoring. Seeing her book they had come across the way of taking the stress out of motoring and leaving it to someone else! She took out her excursion book and told him she had an almost full coach but she would check with Georg if she could have the 56-seater in which case there would be room for them. After phoning, she returned to the bar with the news that they could join the trip. Tall Father was delighted, paid up straight away and asked her to join them for a drink, which she did. 'I'm afraid I cannot stay very long as I have to escort my guests to the slide show, but I will be here tomorrow at six-thirty to give you the brochures so you can familiarise yourselves with what lies in store on your trip.' Amelia intrigued Tall Mother. She said she had never met a rep before, as they had never been on a package holiday. They had always travelled privately, but they were all looking forward to having a new experience.

The highlight of Amelia's week was the trek up to the Alm. It was another cloud-free, warm day with not a breath of wind. She was glad of her hiking boots as it was so important to have the right sort of footwear for the slippery incline on the loose shingle as they made their way up to the Alm, hand in hand. Marcus was brilliant company and chatted away about the village and villagers he so loved. He had a wicked sense of humour as well as being a bit of a tease, and as they progressed further and further up the mountain through the dense woods, Amelia knew that, for the first time in her life, she was deeply in love! She was in another world, one she was perfectly happy in and oblivious of yesterdays and tomorrows.

They reached the Alm and were met by an overjoyed Luggi the farmer, who was a lifelong best buddy of Marcus. They sat outside with a large beer, Schnapps, and the traditional home-made bread with cheese and ham. Luggi joined them in between serving the other hikers, then called for his son to bring the squeezebox and join them. It was such a wonderful relaxed atmosphere, as Franz played accompanied by his father on the guitar. The other customers who were all German or Austrian sang their hearts out. In the background and not very far away they could hear the cowbells as the cows grazed on the lush green grass, a picture of contentment and serenity.

The time went too quickly and soon it was time for the descent. Amelia felt reluctant to leave this beautiful tranquil spot but her duty called. They took their leave with a promise they would return soon and once again hand in hand started their return journey.

'Did you enjoy your trip to the Alm, *Millilein?*' asked Marcus, with feeling in his voice.

She responded, and surprised him and herself as she gave him a peck on the cheek.

They looked at each other seriously, then Marcus cupped her face in his hands and kissed her very gently on the lips, and as if it was the most natural thing in the world to do, she responded.

They sat on a tree stump and Marcus poured out his feelings for her. Amelia could fight it no longer and finally admitted she felt the same.

'Marcus, we must keep this to ourselves until the season is over and then we can have some quality time together. You do understand my work comes first and I cannot risk having distractions, as I have a full work load as you already know, but we can carry on as normal and get together whenever I have some free time.'

Marcus was so in love he would have agreed to anything! The time was getting very near for her office hours and they almost had to run to get there in time.

Jill was surprised to see her without her badges and in hiking boots, so it was obvious she had not been home after the Alm. One look at Amelia's face told her everything: her friend was in love – not that she was unaware before, but now it looked like it had gone a step further.

'Jill, I have had one of the happiest days of my life,'

she said seriously but with a glow about her Jill had never seen before.

'It shows all over your face. But where do you go from here?' she asked, equally as serious.

'I really don't know. What I do know is I cannot and will not fight it any more, it's in the lap of the gods. But one thing is certain, I will not let my feelings interfere with my work.'

'I think you will find that easier said than done, but you can count on me. I would be the last person to deny you any happiness especially in my situation with Richard,' said Jill, putting her arm around her friend's shoulder. They lifted their glasses and made a toast. 'To the future! Whatever is thrown at us!' they said in unison.

Later, lying in bed and going over the day's events, Amelia was annoyed with herself for being so full of her wonderful day that she had forgotten to thank Jill for taking her trip and looking after her guests, who had told her at the office hours how much they had enjoyed it. With a picture of that special smile and those laughing green eyes in her mind, she contentedly fell asleep.

On the return from the Innsbruck/Italy trip, Tall Father and his family positively gushed about the fantastic experience it had been and about how it had completely opened their eyes to the advantages of a package holiday. Tall Mother said, 'Do you know Amelia, we have been coming to the Tirol for the past seventeen years – this being the first but not the last trip to Bachl – and we have learnt more in one day than the whole time we have been coming. We all want to thank you for making the trip possible and your wonderful commentary and wondered if there is any room for us on the Salzburg trip?'

Amelia once again promised she would see what she could do. Feeling very pleased with herself she carried on with her office hours. Marcus popped by and asked her to meet him in the Alpenhof after her evening entertainment was over. She nodded and gave a faint smile as she looked into his lovely eyes. This did not go unnoticed by the locals who had all guessed there was something more than friendship there – it was the biggest open secret in the village! With a spring in her step and looking forward to seeing him again she walked into the Alpenhof expecting to see Marcus at the bar and was temporarily disappointed to find he was not there. Scanning the room she caught sight of him sitting at a corner table with several other people.

On approaching him she was horrified to see his companions were the Swedish crowd, including Leni! Before she had chance to turn around, Marcus had seen her and beckoned her over. She had a fixed smile on her face as he introduced her to the group, oblivious to her unease. Leni stood up and held her hand out saying, 'Nice to meet you, but I'm sure I saw you here last year.'

'That's right, I have been here over a year now, but I can't remember seeing you,' lied Amelia, feeling extremely awkward.

'This is my husband Sven. It's his first time in Bachl. This is a sort of belated honeymoon for us,' Leni said, looking lovingly at her husband.

'Congratulations,' said Amelia a little too enthusiastically, as relief flooded through her.

Marcus drew up a chair next to him as he called the waitress over to order her a wine. She sat next to him and responded to his hand squeeze under the table. The Swedes were such a nice crowd and by the end of the evening she felt she had known them for years, and was full of remorse over her previous thoughts of them as the enemy! Leni told her she had been coming to Bachl for many years and always stayed with Marcus's family. She had put her arm around Marcus's shoulder as she

159

said to Amelia, 'I love this man, and he has always been like a big brother to me!' Marcus looked faintly embarrassed at this outburst of affection and said with a laugh, 'You have someone else to look after you on your holidays now.'

Afterwards, as he walked Amelia the short distance to her flat, he said, 'I meant everything I said to you on the Alm you know, *Millilein.*'

'I know, and so did I, but I was really taken aback when I saw you with Leni tonight as I was given to understand that you and her had been an item,' she said, almost questioningly.

'Leni is a terrible flirt but we have nothing in common except our love of Gasthofs and hiking. Apart from that she is like a kid sister, but we both knew people were putting two and two together and making five so we just let them carry on believing it. I am happy she has found a good man, as she was a bit of a lonely soul,' he said in earnest.

Amelia did not dare tell him of her feelings when she saw them together but instead gave him a big bear hug before she slipped quietly indoors.

24

Amelia tried once again to phone Luc but was told by his secretary that he was still away on business. Amelia had missed their Friday afternoons together and wondered if she should tell him about Marcus, but knowing he would not approve decided against it. She did not want to spoil a beautiful friendship. On the other hand she could not tell Marcus about Luc as there was no way he would understand it was platonic! Even so, she was very fond of Luc and felt uncomfortable with the thought that something was troubling him.

Jill had been counting the days to the arrival of Richard, and Amelia was just dying to meet her friend's 'hero'. She was not disappointed, as Jill swept arm in arm with him into the Jagerhof. He was tall like Jill, with a craggy handsomeness attributed to someone who spent a lot of time outdoors. He was absolutely charming and had eyes for no one but Jill. As for Jill, her lovely face was a picture of adoration as she hung onto his every word. The locals had been somewhat curious as they had known her for years and always had the impression she was a bit standoffish with no time for men. She was very popular and respected by them for her professional attitude towards her work, so it came as a bit of a surprise to see her so lovingly tender towards her boyfriend. Jill must have told him about Marcus, as he suggested that the four of them went for a meal sometime. Amelia looked at Jill who nodded approval and said it was a great idea; they would have to work out which night would be the best. That didn't take long as the only evening they finished reasonably early was Saturday – arrivals day – and after they had finished their office hours. Amelia was quite excited at the prospect as it would be the first time they would be together in public as a couple. She had decided not to care what anyone thought any more. This is my life and my business, and I am doing exactly what I want, she thought. She could not help but be more than a little worried about her parents' reaction, but thought again 'I'll worry about that when the time comes!' When Marcus arrived in the bar she introduced him to Richard as if it were the most natural thing in the world to do. Marcus was pleasantly surprised to find Amelia was making no effort to keep their feelings for each other a secret any longer, and agreed enthusiastically to a meal together. By the end of the evening the happy foursome had decided on the 'Wiederberg' at Innerbachl for their meal the following Saturday evening.

On the return from Italy to Innsbruck the following week, an elderly lady made her way to the front of the coach and whispered in Amelia's ear, 'I'm sorry to trouble you dear, but I think my husband has died!' Amelia sat bolt upright and seeing the concern on the old lady's face whispered back, 'I will make my way up the bus in a few minutes on the pretence I am just making sure everyone has their passports ready for the passport control at the border. Do you think you can stay calm so as to not alert anyone else, especially the border guards, until we are safely back in Austria? Once we're over the border I will get in touch with my boss who will have help at hand.'

'Yes of course dear, I am just sorry to cause you all this trouble.'

'Please do not apologise, Mrs Roberts. I promise you everything that can be done will be done as soon as we are over the border,' said Amelia feeling so sorry for this gentle, humble, elderly lady. Inwardly the panic was beginning to manifest itself at the thought of the border guards noticing anything untoward, as it meant the bus would be grounded and everyone stuck in Italy with masses of red tape surrounding a death on their side of the border. She could not bear to think of the consequences!

After a few minutes she slowly walked up the aisle, telling everybody to get their passports ready, as they would be at the border in ten minutes. When she got to Mr and Mrs Roberts' seat about halfway up the bus she was relieved to see Mr Roberts was actually next to the window, with his head on his wife's shoulder. Amelia looked straight at Mrs Roberts and then at her husband who appeared to be sleeping peacefully. Mrs Roberts' eyes said it all, he was well and truly dead!

'To save you disturbing your husband if you let go of his hand, shall I get your passports out ready for you?' Amelia said in as normal a voice as she could manage. The old lady gave her the handbag, which was tucked in between herself and her husband, whilst continuing to hold his hand. The other passengers had no clue of the tragedy that had unfolded and happily held their passports ready for inspection. She did not tell Rudi the driver, as the suspicious guards were quick to pick up any sign of uneasiness.

Amelia had her heart in her mouth as the bus stopped and the guards stepped on board and made their way up the bus looking at each passport. She hoped she hadn't appeared over friendly as she welcomed them aboard but nearly had a fit when they stopped and looked at Mr Roberts. 'Shall I wake him up for you dear?' said Mrs Roberts sweetly and made as if to move. The guard touched her shoulder and said, 'That will not be necessary Signora' and carried on checking everyone else's passports.

Amelia could feel her heart thumping and her palms sweating by the time they finally left and waved the driver on. Thank God! And what a wonderful woman Mrs Roberts was to offer to wake him up and being so confident they would not call her bluff, thought Amelia, full of admiration. Now they had to go through it all again with the Austrian border guards two hundred feet away. As luck would have it they just asked Amelia if all the passengers were British and, with her nod, waved the bus through. She asked Rudi to stop by the phone box as she had to make a call. She told her passengers she would only be a few moments and asked them not to leave the coach, as they would be in Innsbruck in half an hour. After explaining the situation to Anne-Marie she was told that an ambulance would be waiting at the drop-off point in Innsbruck and that Anne-Marie would be there to take over, but she needed three-quarters of an hour to make sure both she and the ambulance would be there. She went on to tell Amelia to give the passengers a ten-minute photo stop at the Bergisl mountain, which was on the outskirts of Innsbruck. Once everyone was off the coach she could put Mrs Roberts in the picture about what was going to happen and assure her that Anne-Marie would be with her the whole time at the hospital and make any arrangements that were needed regarding getting in touch with her family, etc.

Amelia carried out the instructions and on arrival in Innsbruck she saw Anne-Marie with the ambulance parked a discreet distance from the coach stop in order to give the passengers time to get off without arousing suspicion. Rudi had been blissfully unaware of the drama but when Amelia explained the sudden arrival of the ambulance pulling up next to his coach, the colour drained from his face. Seeing this, Amelia thought had he known beforehand, one look at his face would have aroused suspicion of the border guards and this would have been a completely different scenario! The lovely gentle old lady had no thought for herself and her loss, but was more concerned and apologetic at putting everyone to so much trouble. She kissed Amelia's cheek and thanked her again for being so calm and helpful in a very difficult situation and was led by Anne-Marie – an arm about her shoulder – to the car that would take her to the hospital.

Amelia explained their absence to the passengers as Mr Roberts having been taken ill and taken to hospital. She would tell them in a few days that he had passed away in hospital, in order not to alarm them if they knew they had shared the coach with a dead person. Feeling very sad and deflated she was glad for the privacy of her own flat, even though it was only for a short time before her office hours. She sat down and cried her heart out, partly from shock but mostly for that dear unselfish old lady who had a very traumatic time ahead of her. She wished she could talk to Jill right at that moment, to unburden the events of the day. Jill always had words of comfort and wisdom. Then she remembered she would not be seeing her after office hours, as she would be with Richard and on one of their walks away from the village. She was looking forward to seeing Marcus, as she so badly needed a hug.

The office hours seemed to drag and Amelia found it extremely difficult with such a heavy heart to act her normal self, but to ensure her guests did not guess that anything was wrong she managed to stay on top of it. She was never so relieved as when Marcus came and joined her for the last five minutes – to make sure she did not over run her time! He noticed that she was rather subdued, and as she put her books away and cleared up she said, 'Marcus can we go for a walk somewhere?' Fearing she had changed her mind about him he carried her briefcase and led her outside. 'What's up *Millilein*? What's troubling you?' he asked, looking questioningly in her eyes. She took his arm and snuggled up close. 'I'll tell you while we walk,' she said.

Over the space of the next ten minutes she told him in detail what had happened and became distraught when she mentioned seeing Mr Roberts' dead and peaceful face. She had never seen a dead body before. It didn't take Marcus long to realise that although she had remained calm and focused at the time, it had now hit her. He put her briefcase down, wrapped his arms around her and let her sob.

'My poor darling, I am so proud of you to have coped so well, so just let it out now. If it would make you feel any better, let's go into the church and say a prayer for Mrs Roberts as she is the one who is going to need the help. Mr Roberts is at peace and passed over in the perfect way, but its always dreadful for the one left behind.'

Amelia stopped sobbing and stared at him for a moment. 'You are so wise Marcus, and just what I needed at the right time. I feel much better already and would love to visit the church.'

As they entered the beautiful ornate old church Amelia immediately felt a deep sense of peace. Churches always had this effect on her. They sat with their heads bowed and silently prayed. She was unaware that Marcus's prayers were quite different from hers but with the same deep feeling. They sat up and his hand found hers.

'I could never love you more than I do at this moment *Millilein*. I hope the day will come when I can look after you forever,' he said very seriously.

'What a lovely thing to say Marcus, you really are an old romantic and softie at heart and I love you very much for it.'

'Let's go for a drink *Millilein*. I think you must be ready for one as I certainly know that I am!'

It was not until that moment that Amelia realised how much he had come to mean to her and no matter what was thrown at them they were going to be together, come hell or high water!

They sat on the balcony of the Alpenhof, oblivious to some sideways glances, one being from Franz Rissbacher who on seeing them together was left in no doubt they were indeed now a couple. In the distance Amelia saw Jill and Richard coming down the road with arms around each other and beckoned them over. Jill immediately noticed Amelia's shiny face and smudged eye make up. 'What's up Mel? Have you been crying?' she said, rather shocked by her friend's appearance.

'I'm all right now Jill, but I have had one hell of a day,' said Amelia and carried on relating the whole story.

'Oh my God! You have experienced every rep's worst nightmare!' said Jill who had listened open-mouthed.

'Marcus has been a wonderful shoulder to lean on. Without his words of wisdom I think I would have totally lost it even though I kept perfectly calm at the time – well on the outside anyway. It only really hit me after I dropped my guests off. I just seemed to go to pieces. I found it extremely difficult trying to appear normal at my office hours but I'm afraid afterwards when I met Marcus and tried to tell him I just could not control the tears any more. I'm all right now but it was such a relief to talk about it. Poor Marcus, he caught the whole sobbing part of it, it was such a relief to let it out.'

Richard ordered some more drinks and the foursome sat on the balcony and chatted as if they had known each other all their lives, until darkness closed in.

25

August was fast approaching, and all the reps were beginning to feel the strain of the long hours spent taking excursions and the evening entertainment programme. Jill was very upset after Richard had left, and much as she would have liked to spend more time with her, Amelia also had Marcus to consider. She found that actually seeing him after a day's work helped her cope, instead of it being a distraction as she had originally wrongly thought it might. She was surprised – but not greatly – when Jill breathlessly told her that Richard had proposed while they were at the airport and what's more she had accepted. Amelia flung her arms around her and said genuinely that she was delighted and very happy for her.

'We reckon we have known each other long enough Mel, and I shall be thirty next birthday and Richard thirty-five, so I think that any wild oats have now been sown and we are both ready for a commitment. It's funny how it all happened, as I had given up on finding the man of my dreams. Then out of the blue and when I was least expecting it there was Richard!'

'Does this mean you won't be doing the winter season Jill?' asked Amelia with a sinking feeling.

'Afraid so. My contract is due to be signed next week so I shall tell my boss then that this is my last season. I shall miss you Mel, but it has taken so long to find each other we do not want to spend any more time apart,' she said, giving Amelia a big sister-like hug. This seemed a good time to ask Amelia about her plans.

'Quite frankly Jill, I cannot envisage a life without Marcus and I know there will be a lot of obstacles, the biggest being his religion as there is no way I would convert to Catholicism. That would mean that I would not be recognised by his church as his wife were we to have a Protestant marriage in Innsbruck.'

'Well that is an obstacle you can overcome Mel, but what about this emancipation thing that the womenfolk here do not have? Never in a million years would you put up with your husband being out all hours, especially in the ski season, knowing what you do!'

Amelia smiled and said she had spoken about this in great depth with Marcus, who pointed out that he would not expect her to behave as a village wife and that he also respected her religion. He was quite prepared for a Protestant marriage and its complications as far as his religion was concerned. All that mattered to them both was being together. 'We will decide exactly what we are going to do before the summer is over. Then I have the difficult job of convincing my parents I am doing the right thing. But I know that once they meet him their minds will be put at rest,' said Amelia.

'Do they have any idea what is on their doorstep Mel?'

'Not a clue Jill, I have never mentioned him. I just want to tell them face to face!'

'Well good luck kiddo, as I think you might need it if your parents are anything like mine!' said Jill earnestly.

Amelia's twenty-fourth birthday came around on the twentieth of August. It was the Krimml waterfalls excursion day and found her in high spirits and enjoying the trip, despite this being the thirteenth time she had done it. Her guests were appreciative and as usual enjoying themselves, but Amelia had a new spring in her step and

169

was so looking forward to seeing Marcus. They had planned a meal out together, as Jill had insisted on taking over her friend's duties at the bowling evening to give them some time to celebrate.

Amelia raced home for a quick change and took more time than usual with her appearance. Satisfied she was looking her best and in her favourite Tirolean dirndl – a blue dress with tight bodice dress and a full skirt adorned with little pink roses, worn over a white blouse with little puff sleeves edged in lace – her stomach did a flip when she saw him stride through the door, his white shirt in stark contrast to his deep tan and dark curly hair. He looked drop-dead gorgeous.

Marcus in return was thinking how lucky he was to have the love of such a beautiful English rose and in traditional Tirolean costume to boot! 'We are going for a little walk before our meal *Millilein*, as I have something to show you,' he said, taking her hand and leading her past some farmhouses and down a little hill.

'This is a part of Bachl I am not familiar with Marcus. Where are we going?' she asked.

'Patience *Millilein*, we are nearly there,' he said with a mysterious smile.

There in front of them was a little wooden bridge spanning a fast-flowing brook. On the far side of the bridge was a forest of dense fir trees, and to the right before the bridge was a picture-postcard wooden chalet. It was so fairytale-like, Amelia would have not been surprised if a cuckoo had popped out above the front door. Marcus led her to the door and reached for the key from behind the bench on the balcony. He opened the door and led her in to the hall where to the left was the kitchen and another door leading onto the balcony facing the woods and overlooking the brook. It had red check curtains at both windows and every piece of furniture

170

was in carved wood. There was a huge wood-burning range and, surprise surprise, a large cuckoo clock on the wall next to the balcony door.

Temporarily unable to speak, she allowed herself to be led through to the living room that again had a door to the balcony that surrounded the house. It was so cosy with its scattered woollen rugs, carved furniture and long settee. Marcus then led her to the big cellar that housed the washing machine and gardening tools and a shower room.

'Who does this belong to Marcus?' she asked, wondering what this was all leading to.

'Come and see the rest first,' he said. Upstairs were two double bedrooms with the traditional big white feather duvets looking like giant marshmallows, wooden wardrobes with religious scenes painted on them, and a door leading to the upstairs balcony. She was surprised to see a bathroom and loo in such an old house and concluded they must have been added quite recently, like the shower in the basement. Marcus opened the balcony door and they stepped outside to the sound of birdsong and the gush of the water flowing past in the brook below.

'This is idyllic Marcus, but why have you brought me here?' she asked, still puzzled.

'My grandfather built this house to be used as a summerhouse, somewhere he could sit and study in the peace and quiet. It was away from the hustle and bustle of the main house with its grocery shop and tailoring business. They also let part of the ground floor there to other traders so he could never have the peace he wanted for his studies, hence he built this little house, which was his salvation. My father, being the eldest son, lived here when he first got married to my mother, but when the children started to come along they had to move back into the big house. Likewise, as the only son of seven children it was passed down to me and because I had no need for it, being unmarried, my eldest sister and her husband lived here for nearly ten years with their three children. But then, last year, Gottfried her husband – who is a builder – finished the hotel that had taken four years to build, and the family moved in. Since then, as all my sisters have their own larger homes, rather than leave it empty it has been used as a holiday let winter and summer.'

Amelia sat on the balcony taking this all in. 'What a lovely story Marcus, they must have all been so happy here. It surprised me that it is much larger than it appears from the outside, and thank you for bringing me and letting me share some of your family history,' she said giving him a peck on the cheek.

He looked at her, his eyes laughing and with the old familiar grin said out of the blue, 'Could you consider this your home after we are married *Millilein*?'

Completely overwhelmed and feeling she was in a dream, she could not answer straight away but on seeing his worried expression she quickly came down to earth and threw herself into his arms. 'I love it, love it, love it, Marcus,' was all she could say.

'Can I take that as a yes then?' he said laughingly as he held her close.

'Oh, yes please, my darling Marcus, I'm just finding it all too wonderful to be true,' she said breathlessly.

'Good, now let's go and celebrate your birthday, I'm starving,' he said as he grabbed her hand and led her down the stairs and to the front door.

'Just a moment please, can I have one last look before we go?' she pleaded.

'Go ahead *Millilein*, we have a little time before our meal so while you are having a good look around I am going to sit on the balcony with one of those beers I spied in the cellar,' said a bemused but happy Marcus.

She wandered from room to room, taking in the beauty of each one, which had been so lovingly thought out. This is the dearest little home I have ever been in and I just know we are going to be so happy here, she thought, still completely overwhelmed. She joined Marcus on the balcony and shared his beer.

'*Millilein*, I've been thinking, now that you have been here, do you think it would be a good idea for you to tell your parents when you go home in September? They are going to be surprised, but will they accept it?'

'Of course they will, but you must come over to meet them and put their minds at rest' was her reply.

'How about if I come early October? It will give them the chance to realise we are serious and perhaps then we can make arrangements to get married in Innsbruck in November. It's my birthday on the ninth and that would be the ultimate in birthday presents.' He paused before adding, 'At least I will never have an excuse to forget our anniversary!' He looked hopefully at Amelia, waiting for her answer.

'This has all happened a bit fast Marcus. I want the same as you, but you do realise I have signed my contract for the winter season and cannot be a stay-at-home wife.'

'I would not expect you to give your work up *Millilein*, unless you wanted to. This arrangement will suit us both and I certainly would not want to go so often to the Gasthofs having you to come home to! I shall tell my family our plans at the right time but I know even though they will not warm to the idea of a Protestant wedding they will be relieved to see me settle down, and with such a gentle lovely wife. They already have great admiration for you and even though they don't say very much, they know and have known how I feel about you for a long time, so it will come as no surprise.'

They sat eating their meal and going over and over

their plans. It all made a lot of sense. Lying in her bed much later, Amelia said a little prayer and thanked God for the most wonderful birthday of her life and prayed for His help and guidance for their future. She was so excited, it was hours before she fell asleep with a smile on her face, and it was still there when she awoke the next morning!

After many attempts to get through to Luc, he finally answered the phone. 'I have been trying for weeks to get you Luc but your secretary said you were away on business. Is everything ok?'

'Yes, I'm fine thanks. How are you? Will you be in Innsbruck on Friday?'

Amelia thought he sounded a bit flat but told him she would meet him at the same time and in the same place and how she was looking forward to seeing him as she had some news.

'I look forward to that Amelia. Cheers!' he said before putting the phone down.

Amelia was not looking forward to it, as she knew she had to tell him about Marcus and she knew his views on village men were not exactly complimentary. Luc meant a lot to her as he was someone she could trust and talk about anything with. She admired him and their friendship meant a lot to her. He had a brilliant sense of humour and always treated her like a lady. She put Luc out of her mind, which was not difficult as she was full of the excitement of getting married. It would be a relief when Marcus actually told his family of their plans and she hoped there would not be too much fuss over their venue for the celebration.

She met Luc as planned and went once again to their usual restaurant in the palace gardens. He had noticed already that even though she was a strikingly lovely-looking woman she now had a certain glow about her. 'Come on then, what's this news you have for me?' he asked looking amused.

Amelia watched the frown appear as she unfolded all that had happened and looked pleadingly at him hoping for his approval. Luc was certainly taken aback, but on seeing how soft she became every time she mentioned Marcus, he could not be churlish and voice his disapproval. She was obviously deeply in love and he knew even though it was a selfish thought that this would alter their relationship – despite Amelia assuring him it wouldn't. She didn't know the village men as he did!

'I hope you will be very happy Amelia, but please remember I will always be your friend and if ever you need anything you know you can count on me,' was all he said, and she knew he meant every word of it. They said their goodbyes, and planned to meet the following Friday as usual.

As Amelia happily went back to the coach, Luc went for a walk around the palace gardens. He had a heavy heart; not only due to Amelia's news but also because of the trouble he had had recently with his secretary. He had not been away on business at all, and unfortunately every time Amelia had rung she had not passed the messages on, so he had no idea of her phone calls. He had sadly thought that Amelia did not want to meet up again. Why had Elspet not put through Amelia's calls? He knew the answer, but had not realised before that she was jealous. Did she think he would not find out? His mind was in turmoil and he did not look forward to his return to the office and the confrontation. She had been with him for eight years, and was not only a first-class secretary but also someone he counted on. They had been on many dinner dates but he had always made it clear that it was on a friendship basis and nothing else – which she had seemed to accept, but obviously from her actions, had not! It also unnerved him in having to admit to himself that he felt more than friendship for Amelia and had hoped that one day it might have developed into something more. Her news had devastated him, as he had no idea she had feelings for Marcus.

There were tears and apologies from Elspet as she poured out her love for Luc, but on hearing Amelia was getting married she begged to keep her job, and promised to keep her distance and feelings in check. Lucien was not so sure but against his better judgement agreed to give it a try for a month on a professional basis. As far as Elspet was concerned, regardless of her promises she could still see a light at the end of the tunnel and vowed to make herself discreetly indispensable. She was convinced that one day he would love her too – especially now that Amelia was out of the frame. The only obstacle now was his Italian girlfriend, as far as she knew!

After the band concert on Friday evening, Marcus joined the reps on the Jagerhof balcony. He had asked Amelia not to mention their plans until he had told his family, which he was going to over dinner on Saturday. By now the reps had known for weeks just by observing their eye contact and body language that Marcus and Amelia were most definitely an item, so it would come as no surprise when the engagement was announced. Being as it was a lovely warm evening and with more than an hour of daylight left, Marcus suggested they went for a walk down to the summerhouse as he knew she was dying to have another look. They were sitting on the balcony drinking a beer when Marcus put his hand in his pocket and told Amelia to close her eyes. He picked up her hand and she felt a ring go on her engagement finger. Her eyes flew open and she just stared at her hand. She had a big lump in her throat and felt tears sting her eyes and then roll down her cheeks. Startled, Marcus said 'Don't you like it *Millilein*?'

'I just love it Marcus, I just love it!' she said trying to pull herself together. The ring was an engraved band of gold, which was traditional to Austria, and it fitted her perfectly.

'We will make our engagement public on Sunday, so keep it on your necklace chain until then my darling *Millilein*,' he said, holding her very close. He disappeared indoors and brought back two glasses and a bottle of ice-cold pink champagne. Intertwining their arms, they made the toast 'To us' and stayed until darkness fell and the champagne bottle drained.

'Much as I would love to stay here with you I have the airport run tomorrow and an early start, so it's about time I went home, not that I am expecting to sleep, dear Marcus!' The next day Amelia found her hand often going to the ring on the gold chain around her neck, a secret smile appearing each time. She would have loved to have told her colleagues at the airport but it would have to wait until the next week. She knew Jill would say nothing so it was going to come as a surprise both to them and to Anne-Marie.

She couldn't wait to get back to the village and meet up with Marcus after her office hours to find out the result of his announcement of their engagement to his family, and she was more than a little relieved to see the smile on his face as he stood at the bar waiting for her.

'They were very happy until I told them where we were getting married and why, but relented when they could see it was not open to discussion. But they do expect that when we have children they will be brought up as Catholics,' he said seriously. She found his hand, squeezed it and told him they would worry about that when the time came, to which he nodded in agreement.

'Tomorrow, *Millilein*, we will announce it after your welcome meeting as there will be many of the locals here after the church service so it would be a good opportunity.'

177

The next big obstacle would be telling her parents, but she had decided she would definitely not do that until she was back in Exeter. She put it to the back of her mind and felt butterflies in her tummy thinking about the next day and actually being able to wear her ring. He met her the next day as planned, took the ring from the chain around her neck and placed it on her finger. In the packed bar he called for hush and made the announcement. There were people coming from all directions to shake their hands and uttering their congratulations. Marcus and Amelia just stood there and beamed. There were also several of Amelia's guests who had witnessed this and who were visibly delighted and they too offered their congratulations. It was all like a dream.

The Innsbruck/Italy trip seemed to come around quickly and found Amelia sitting with Luc in their usual restaurant. He picked up her hand and looked at the ring. 'Does this mean it's official now Amelia?' he asked, trying to sound pleased. She nodded and told him of their plans. 'It's all moving a bit fast, but if you are sure this is what you want then you have my congratulations and I hope you will be very, very happy. If there is ever anything, and I mean anything I can ever do for you, you just have to pick up the phone, I want you to remember that,' he said earnestly.

'Thank you Luc, I appreciate your sincerity, but please believe me, I am going into this with my eyes wide open. I have no intention of giving up my existing friends, and Marcus would not expect me to! And being as I am going to carry on working for BA I hope we can meet up in the winter on my Innsbruck excursions as usual.'

They sat chatting away, quite comfortable in each other's company until it was time to meet the coach. 'Next week, same time?' she asked, smiling.

'I shall be here for you Amelia as normal.' Then as an afterthought he said, 'When are you planning on returning to the UK?'

'In about three weeks' time, so I shall be seeing you a few more times before I leave and probably bore you with my wedding plans!' she laughed. He kissed her cheek and they parted.

When Amelia told Jill how touched she had been by Luc's concern over how fast everything was going, Jill didn't dare tell her that Luc had only voiced how she herself felt – but seeing her friend's happiness she only said that Amelia was fortunate to have such a reliable good friend – and a very attractive one to boot! They arranged to go into Innsbruck to sort out a wedding outfit in two weeks' time when they had both seen their last guests off. The shops in Innsbruck were fantastic and there was a wide choice of beautiful clothes shops. Jill said how sorry she was not to be able to be there for the wedding, but it would be impossible to get back over between seasons. Amelia understood this and promised there would be lots of photos that she would send and they would always, always be best friends and never lose touch. 'Come on, we're getting a bit emotional here! Let's go and have a drink before the bowling,' Amelia said linking her arm through Jill's.

Marcus met her on her return from the bowling alley and Amelia told him of the plan she had made with Jill about her wedding dress. It would be something really lovely but definitely not a white wedding. 'Whatever you want *Millilein* is fine by me. I am going in to see the Registrar on Monday and book the ninth November. Are you happy, *Millilein?*' he asked, but did not need a reply, the dreamy look on her face said it all. 'Next Wednesday I shall be in Innerbachl all day as it is the annual woodcutting day and I shall be collecting the winter supply

179

of logs both for the main house and summerhouse for us.' She looked at him and asked him whom he would be going with. He explained that there would be four of them and that they helped each other with the felling and chopping, that every family owned a certain amount of trees and for every one cut a new one would be planted. It was an arduous task but one they all enjoyed with their packed lunches and liquid refreshment!

At the airport the reps had already heard on the grapevine of her engagement and were giving her hugs. Anne-Marie was thrilled, especially as she knew Amelia would be carrying on repping and was delighted to hear that she was invited to the wedding. There was no time to answer all the questions being fired at Amelia about the venue, her dress, where she was going to live... She avoided the answer when she was asked what her parents thought, she tried to keep that one blip at the back of her mind, but was sure that when they met Marcus they would be won over. She waited nervously after her office hours on Monday to hear the result of Marcus's visit to the Registrar. She needn't have worried – as soon as she saw his broad grin she knew that everything was going according to plan.

'All organised *Millilein*, 11 am Friday the ninth of November.' He produced an official-looking document and there in black and white were their names and the date of the nuptials. It had been so fortunate she had her birth certificate with her as it would have been extremely awkward to have written to her mother to ask for it to be sent on without having to give a reason, and she did not like the thought of making up some cock and bull story, but on the other hand she could not tell her the truth. That she could only do face to face, to ease them gently into the idea. Anyway that problem had not arisen so she didn't know why she was even thinking about it! She was so blissfully happy and had so much to look forward to. Nothing could dampen her spirits.

26

The Salzburg trip was one she really did not enjoy. It was a 7 am start, with the sun in her eyes for the three-hour journey there and after a three-hour stay she would have the sun in her eyes all the way back. This was one time she did not enjoy sitting up front in the well of the bus with the driver, but her guests always loved it and were always inspired by the beauty of the city. They never minded the long journey, but for the reps it became a bit of a chore when they had done it week in and week out all season long. She was always glad when she had Heinz as the driver as he was great company – a bit of a tease but always in high spirits. She met up with other reps, some from different companies, at a little café that was the reps' haunt. They found the time passed by much quicker over coffee and gateaux and telling each other about their week, this week's topic being Amelia's engagement. Even though it was early September it was still very warm and quite humid. She was glad to get back to the air-conditioned coach.

Her guests were nearly all there but the bus was still locked and no sign of Heinz, which was unusual. He suddenly appeared and without greeting her as he usually did he got on the coach and started the engine. 'Everything all right Heinz?' she asked a little concerned to see his worried expression.

'Yes, Yes everything fine Milli,' he replied, but it was obvious that it was not. She checked all her guests were there and told him they were ready for departure. She picked up the microphone, asked if everyone had enjoyed their day and explained that as they had to go back the same way they had come there would be no more commentary but that she was putting the tape of 'The Sound of Music' for them to relax to. She looked again at Heinz and wondered what had upset him, so once again asked if anything was troubling him. 'No, no Milli, I am fine,' was all he would say. She wondered if perhaps he had a row with his wife, as she knew he always rang her when he reached his destination on his excursions. Whatever it was he was not prepared to talk about it but it must be something serious as his face was a picture of misery. 'Well it's not my business, there is obviously some private matter that he cannot discuss with me,' she thought, but it disturbed her to see this man she was very fond of and also one of Marcus's best friends so completely uncharacteristically quiet.

It was a longer than usual trip back without Heinz's banter. She decided not to try making conversation, as he obviously was not in the mood. As they turned off the Autobahn at Bergbrucke and started the descent up the Bachl valley, Amelia could see the afternoon's storm clouds gathering overhead. During late summer it was not unusual for thunderstorms to occur on an almost daily basis, the rain providing a welcome relief to the humid and muggy weather that built up during the day.

By the time the coach neared the end of the valley, where it started its final climb up to Bachl itself, the thunderstorm was in full swing. The skies had darkened, thunder clapped overhead and echoed around the mountains, whose shadows were illuminated by the sheet lightning, and the rain was coming down torrentially. Halfway up she was glad to see Jill was outside her flat in a mac and scurrying towards the coach for a lift up to the village. Heinz opened the passenger door and instead of Jill getting in she stood on the road and yelled over the noise of the thunder and rain.

'Can you get off Mel, I need to have a chat.'

Puzzled, Amelia replied to her friend they could chat in the village after she had seen her guests off, but Jill responded, 'Please get off Mel, Heinz will see the passengers safely off.' Amelia quickly realised something was seriously wrong and with wobbly legs asked if her parents were all right.

'Yes, yes Mel, your parents are fine, please come with me to my flat now.'

Amelia ran speechlessly after Jill. Once inside, Jill took off her mac and handed her a glass of brandy, insisting Amelia took a big swig before she told her what was wrong. Jill quickly poured one for herself, took a big gulp and before she could say anything Amelia, almost hysterical, said, 'It's Marcus isn't it? Has he had an accident?'

Jill nodded, and choked the words out. He had been killed whilst tree cutting.

'No, no it can't be, there must be some mistake, he's an experienced woodcutter,' Amelia almost screamed.

Jill held her close and told her it had been a tragic accident, a tree had fallen the wrong way and killed him instantly. He didn't know anything about it, and it could not have been prevented, they had adhered to the strict rules, it was just a horrible fluke and had never ever happened before.

Amelia was in total shock as Jill told her it had happened mid-morning and the whole village was in mourning. Her hands were icy cold, she felt as if she was in some terrible nightmare and hoped she would wake up soon. She started to whimper and then broke out into uncontrolled sobbing. Jill was also red-eyed and trying so hard to be strong for her dear friend.

Amelia sobbed, 'Now I know what was wrong with Heinz, it must have been hell for him having to keep that from me for so long. Where is Marcus now?'

Jill told her very gently that he was in the Chapel of Rest at the church.

'I must go to him straight away Jill.'

'Wait! Wait! Mel, I am coming with you. Please finish that brandy then we'll go together.'

Amelia downed it in one go and much as she wanted to run she found she was taking slow steps with Jill's arm around her.

The whole atmosphere in the village was so subdued and quiet, and she never noticed the villagers she passed who with red eyes looked pitifully at her. The thunderstorm had eased off, leaving the air clear and fresh. On turning the last corner, the church came into sight and she saw immediately the coffin surrounded by wreaths with a long queue of people already paying their last respects. They stood to one side as they saw Jill and Amelia approach and as if in a dream Amelia stood silently at the foot of the coffin. Through her tears she saw the large photo. It was a close-up of Marcus with his half smile and laughing green eyes, and was placed on top of the coffin next to a large wreath. The reality hit her and hit her hard.

'Oh no! Please no!' she wailed before she felt her knees buckling underneath her. Jill quickly held her up as Franz Rissbacher suddenly appeared and helped her take Mel into the church. There was so much sadness, it was surreal. Amelia was in a total state of shock and in between sobs asked how Marcus's family were.

'It has hit them all dreadfully, especially his mother and father who doted on their only son,' Franz told her, himself a picture of total disbelief.

'I must go to them Jill. Would you please come with me?'

Jill nodded and still with their arms linked they left the church and slowly made their way past the silent crowd. Marcus's whole family were at the big house and each one embraced Amelia without saying a word, their faces said it all. They could hear Marcus's mother sobbing before they actually saw her, sitting with her husband's arm around her shoulders. Amelia's heart went out to them and she knelt at their feet and took Gertraud's hand, which was also icy cold. The old lady looked up, grief-stricken, her eyes red and swollen. 'My son is dead, Milli,' she said in between sobs and began rocking to and fro.

'I know Gertraud, I know,' said Amelia nearly choking on her words. She could find no words to say. No words of comfort came into her head. She just squeezed the old lady's hand, and in a loving gesture patted her husband's shoulder gently, then got up to leave. His sisters all embraced her again. No words were needed as everyone was united in their grief.

'I cannot do my office hours Jill, I just want to go back to my flat.'

'Shush Mel, shush. That has all been taken care of. I have spoken to Anne-Marie and she is coming up to Bachl tomorrow. Your office hours have been taken care of and Anne-Marie said to forget about work, you are not expected to do anything except look after yourself. We have organised your trips out between us and I am going to stay with you tonight.'

'You are such a pal Jill. Whatever would I have done without you today? I just cannot take it in!'

At Amelia's flat Jill produced a bottle of brandy out of her briefcase, poured two glasses and joined Amelia on the balcony. It was such a beautiful evening with the sound of cowbells, birdsong, and a distant tractor harvesting. Everything was the same as yesterday except for the profound emptiness Amelia felt. It was like her heart had been torn out.

'Why Jill, why? He was so loved and we had such a wonderful future ahead of us and now there is nothing but an empty void all because of one stupid tree.'

Her tears flowed and Jill just let her pour out her heart. After a little while Jill said she was going to get them some sandwiches. Amelia nodded, a vacant smile on her lips and her eyes fixed on Innerbachl across the valley. Jill reappeared with coffee and rolls and not taking no for an answer insisted Amelia ate. 'You have to keep your strength up Mel, it would break Marcus's heart to see you like this all because of him. He is at peace Mel, but he will be tormented knowing your profound unhappiness. He adored you and would want you to be brave,' she said with great authority and conviction.

Amelia looked at her friend and nodded in agreement. 'It is going to be easier said than done. I am so sorry for my selfishness when it has all but destroyed Marcus's parents and family. What are we all going to do without him?' She fell once again into uncontrollable sobbing.

Anne-Marie arrived at the flat at 9.30 the next morning and was shocked to see Amelia who was usually so vibrant now reduced to a picture of grief and with dark shadows under her eyes. 'I am so sorry Amelia, but I want you to know that if there is anything, and I mean anything, I can do to help you have only to ask. I have brought Mariedl with me and she is taking over from you for the rest of the season, she just needs some information and your schedule.'

Amelia nodded, relief etched on her face as she knew she could not socialise, she just wanted to go away and hide but that was not possible until after the funeral was

187

over. Anne-Marie had the unpleasant task of telling her that she had found out all the details of the funeral and as gently as she could, told her it was to be on Saturday at 11 am. Until then, Marcus would remain in the Chapel of Rest. Amelia knew already that it was customary for the deceased to lie in the closed coffin for three days before burial to enable everyone to pay their last respects. Jill had gone on an excursion and Amelia desperately wanted to be near Marcus again so she asked Anne-Marie if she wouldn't mind accompanying her. Wearing her dark sunglasses, she walked arm in arm with Anne-Marie through the village, which was still deadly quiet. She was surprised to see the long line of villagers two and three deep leading up to the Chapel of Rest. She could not cope with joining the queue so asked Anne-Marie to go for a walk with her and she would return after midday when the villagers would be home for their lunch and she could have Marcus to herself. Anne-Marie was only too happy to be of some help.

Amelia led her to a bridge that spanned a fast-flowing brook and standing there she pointed to the pretty little house overlooking the brook. 'That's where we were going to live after we were married,' she said sadly. Anne-Marie smiled wistfully and nodded. They stood for a few more minutes before continuing their walk through the dense fir trees, until they came to a clearing overlooking the village. They sat on an old rustic bench next to a spring, and Amelia suddenly said, 'This was a favourite haunt of Marcus and myself. The times were few and far between because of my work, but we had promised each other we would make up for it during the two weeks after my last guests had left and before I returned Exeter.' She paused and then said, 'Do you know, my parents do not even know of Marcus's existence! I wanted to tell them when I got home, as it would not have been easy trying to put into a letter that not only was I engaged but getting married on the ninth of November to a man they had yet to meet, but I knew that once they had met him when he came over in October their minds would have been put at rest. That is why I wanted to tell them face-to-face. Now they will never know, as I am never going to mention it – it would upset them deeply.'

Anne-Marie listened sympathetically and replied that if she was in Amelia's shoes that is exactly how she would react too. 'I think quite frankly Amelia, once the funeral is over it would be a good idea for you to come straight to Seefeld and stay at my place for a few weeks, as it will give you breathing space before you go back to England.'

Amelia looked surprised, and was touched by Anne-Marie's suggestion. She replied that she had not even thought beyond the funeral but yes, thank you, that would be a godsend.

'Don't make any decisions about the future yet Amelia, as if you find it too painful to come back to Bachl I can allocate you to another resort in the Tirol. Just give yourself a few weeks while you are with me and then you can make a decision.'

'I will always love this village and the villagers and I've come to think of it as my home. But I don't know if I could live here any more as the memory of Marcus would be far too painful. But on the other hand, I could never settle down in England so perhaps this would be the answer.'

'Do not even think of making any decisions yet, just wait for a few weeks and we will go on from there,' said Anne Marie with authority.

Anne-Marie accompanied Amelia to the Chapel of Rest, as it was now way past midday and Amelia had been right – the queue had gone. She was quite taken aback at the amount of flowers, not only surrounding the coffin but also completely filling the chapel with only a single pathway through. With a huge lump in her throat she stared at the photo of the handsome laughing man with twinkling green eyes and was completely overcome. She could quite see how Amelia had fallen for him, his personality shone through. She tried desperately to be strong for Amelia but one look at the crumpled face with tears streaming down her cheeks and Anne-Marie, with tears in her eyes, said, 'He must have been so loved Amelia. I have been many times to a Chapel of Rest but never in my life have I seen so many flowers and so many grieving people.' She took Amelia's arm and led her out through the graveyard.

Amelia said she must go and see Marcus's sister Marianne, who lived nearby. Anne-Marie accompanied her to the house and once seeing the warmth surrounding her there decided it was time to return to Seefeld. She left Amelia and Marianne on the balcony discussing the funeral and after repeating her offer said she would phone on Sunday and arrange to come and pick her up. She gave Amelia a peck on the cheek, shook Marianne's hand and drove away, thinking what she would do without her Robert if anything happened to him. She couldn't get home quickly enough.

The days before the funeral were a blur. Amelia had much support from her close friends in the village and from Jill. Marianne had told her that her husband Erich would come and collect her in the car and bring her to the big family house on Saturday before the funeral. Jill was so relieved to see that the family had taken her into their bosom, as she had to be at the airport. Amelia appeared to have composed herself but was very quiet. Jill's heart went out to her and she wished there was something more she could do to help – then it suddenly dawned on her what she could do.

As if in a daze, Amelia and the family walked immediately behind the coffin, which was carried by six of Marcus's friends, and the whole village in procession followed them. The band led the mourners around the village square playing dirges and there was not a dry eye amongst them. After the service and as the coffin was lowered into the grave Amelia let out a huge uncontrolled sob and cried as if her heart would break. Marcus's sisters, their faces wet with tears, moved closer to her and she felt an arm support her around her waist. The whole reality had suddenly hit her.

After the interment she allowed herself to be led into the Jagerhof, where most of the mourners had gathered. She was placed at the huge reserved family table and together they drank to Marcus. His parents had to be taken home, as they were inconsolable and being both very frail the family feared for their health. After a little while Amelia felt she just wanted to be on her own and after assuring everyone she was all right accepted Erich's offer of a lift home.

Once inside her flat she just collapsed on the bed and the tears flowed until she felt she could cry no more. She sat on the balcony, grateful for the brandy Jill had left, and looked across the valley. It all looked the same; the birds were singing and the cowbells ding-dinging as the cows grazed. She didn't know how long she sat there, but was suddenly aware of a knock on her door. She opened it and came face to face with Lucien!

'Luc? Oh Luc!' she said, completely surprised, and felt his strong arms enveloping her as the tears flowed once again. He stroked her hair and comforted her like a brother. Through her tears she asked how he knew and he replied that Jill had phoned him that morning and told him. 'I was wondering why you never turned up at the palace gardens yesterday and thought that you must have changed your mind. Jill has filled me in with all the details so you don't need to talk about it unless you want to,' he said, still holding her.

Never in her life had she been so happy to see someone, especially Luc, for whom she had great respect. 'Have you eaten, Amelia?' he asked, concerned at the amount of weight she had lost in such a short time.

'I have not been hungry Luc, and I am not hungry now,' she replied.

'Well, young lady, I'm afraid I am taking over for the moment. I think it would be a good idea to get you out of the village, and I just happen to know a very nice little restaurant in the valley where no one knows you, so you will be away from the grieving for a little while and because you must eat.'

Amelia pulled away and seeing the determination in his face decided against protesting. She washed her face but didn't bother with make-up. 'Jill is supposed to be coming up after her office hours and will be wondering where I am if I am not here.' Before she could go any further, Luc interrupted with, 'Jill knows you are with me and said to tell you she will be up for breakfast with you tomorrow, so no more excuses and go and get your jacket.'

Sitting opposite him in the restaurant and forcibly swallowing the food so as not to displease him, she felt a deep sense of relief at being away from the nightmarish preceding days. He listened intently as she told him of her plans to go to Seefeld with Anne-Marie for a few weeks and the alternative she had been given to working in Bachl. Luc told her he had another alternative and that would be to go and work for him in Innsbruck, as his secretary was leaving. There would be a flat that went with the job. Seeing the surprised look on her face, he added seriously that there would be no strings. Amelia smiled and said there was no need to assure her of that, as they were such good friends and she trusted him implicitly.

'Think about it Amelia, it makes sense, as I don't think you would be happy working in another resort and as you have already said you would never be able to settle in England. This would be an ideal solution for both you and me!'

'Dear Luc, I thank you from the bottom of my heart but everything is moving too fast and I cannot think clearly. Please give me a few weeks to get myself back on my feet and I promise I will give you an answer before I go back to Exeter,' she said with feeling.

'Take your time Amelia, and I promise I shall respect your wishes whatever you decide. I shall always be there for you.'

She was so touched by his kindness but her mind was still in turmoil. He drove her back to the village, leaving her still uncertain as to her future.

Epilogue

Three years later, a dark blue Mercedes pulled into the car park adjacent to Bachl church. The door opened and out stepped a man, his wife, and a young child. The man gently kissed his wife and patted the child's head, then stood and watched them as they walked towards the graveyard.

The woman carried a single rose, and holding the child's hand made straight for the far corner. She stopped and stared wistfully at a headstone, placed the rose on the grave, then softly looked at the pretty little girl with chestnut curls and laughing green eyes. She turned back to the grave and tenderly said, 'Hello Marcus. This is Eloise!'